FREDDY *and*
Mr. CAMPHOR

"Ah," he said, and made sweeping motions with the brush.

FREDDY

and

Mr. Camphor

by WALTER R. BROOKS

THE OVERLOOK PRESS
WOODSTOCK & NEW YORK

First published in the United States in 2000 by
The Overlook Press, Peter Mayer Publishers, Inc.
Lewis Hollow Road
Woodstock, NY 12498
www.overlookpress.com

Cataloging-in-Publication Data is available from the Library of Congress.

Manufactured in the United States of America
ISBN 1-58567-027-8
1 3 5 7 9 8 6 4 2

FREDDY *and*
Mr. CAMPHOR

Chapter 1

"I don't know why I perspire so these hot days," said Freddy, the pig. He was sitting on the shady side of the pigpen, fanning himself with a copy of the *Bean Home News*, the newspaper which he had started the summer before for the animals on the Bean farm.

"I expect it's because it's hot," said his Cousin Weedly, who had come over to spend the weekend with him.

"Of course it's because it's hot," said Freddy crossly. "Don't be silly."

"Well, what do you say you don't know for, then?" asked Weedly reasonably. "Either you do or you don't; you can't have it both ways."

"It's because you're too fat," said Jinx, the cat. "Golly, it makes me hot just to look at you, pig, sitting there grunting and mopping your face . . ."

"Oh go away!" Freddy snapped. "My goodness," he said, "haven't you animals got anything better to do than sit around criticizing?"

They looked at each other and Weedly raised his eyebrows—or at least the place where eyebrows would have been if pigs had any—as much as to say: "There now, didn't I tell you?"

"You don't have to bite our heads off," said Jinx.

"Oh dear," said Freddy. "I'm sorry, Jinx. I don't know what's getting into me lately, I'm so cross all the time. It must be the weather. I've never known it to be so hot in April before."

"Unseasonable," said Weedly, nodding his head sagely. "That's what it is—unseasonable. My mother is the same way; it gets on her nerves something terrible."

"And then I've taken so much extra work on

this last year," Freddy went on. "I sometimes think I was much happier when I was just a humble unpolished pig, living in carefree obscurity with no responsibilities on my shoulders. Now, as President of the First Animal Bank, and Editor of the *Bean Home News*, I am continually called upon for all sorts of things. Heading bond drives and addressing bankers' associations and women's clubs . . ." He laid down the paper. "Oh, what a terrible thing is ambition!" he exclaimed. "Why could I not have been content to remain in obscurity, happy in the simple quiet round of daily tasks, busy with my books and my poetry? I might in time have made quite a name for myself as a poet."

"And then you'd have had to address even more societies and women's clubs," said Jinx. "As a matter of fact, you're making a speech now, and when you begin making them even to your friends," he added dryly, "you're in a pretty bad way, if you ask me."

"I think what you need, Cousin Frederick," said Weedly, "is a change."

"Yes," said Freddy gloomily, "I do. But how can I get it? If I take a trip, who'll run the bank and edit the paper?"

"Shut your old bank up for the summer," said

Jinx. "There isn't anything to do there now anyway, since all the animals have drawn their money out and put it into war savings stamps."

"And I'd gather news for the paper and take it to Mr. Dimsey, and he could print it the way he always does," said Weedly. "My mother says I'm always asking a lot of impertinent questions, and that's what a reporter is supposed to do, isn't it?"

"It sounds very nice," said Freddy. "But where could I go? I don't want to travel and have adventures. I'd like to find a nice quiet spot where I could settle down and drowse the long summer hours away. Write a line or two of poetry perhaps, if I felt like it." He looked off dreamily over the freshly ploughed fields of the Bean farm. "Maybe go in bathing to get up an appetite for my supper—there'd have to be water, of course. And then take a short stroll in the gloaming, before climbing in between the cool, lavender-scented sheets." He sighed happily. "I may try my hand at a bit of artistic work —painting, now: I've always felt that I had a talent for painting. Then we can have a show of my work when I come back . . ."

"You haven't gone yet," interrupted Jinx.

"You don't have to be sarcastic," said Freddy

with dignity. "Of course I haven't gone; and as far as I can see I'm not going. Where could I find such a place? I haven't money enough to rent a cottage at a summer resort, and I don't suppose there are many hotels that cater to pigs. So I think—"

"Hey! What's this?" interrupted Weedly. He had been looking at the copy of the *Bean Home News* which Freddy had laid aside, and now he pointed excitedly at an item on the back page.

"Don't interrupt, Weedly," said Freddy reprovingly. "As I was saying . . ."

"But Cousin Frederick!" Weedly insisted. "I'm sorry to interrupt, but this may be just what you're looking for. See here."

So Freddy and Jinx bent over the paper. The item was a small advertisement at the foot of the last page. It read:

WANTED—Reliable party to act as caretaker of large estate during summer. Duties light, remuneration generous. For further details, apply to Mr. Weezer, Pres., First National Bank of Centerboro.

Freddy said, "My goodness, that does look good, doesn't it?" Then he shook his head. "But he'd want a man for that job, not a pig."

"It says 'reliable party,' not 'reliable man,' "

said Jinx. "And if you're not a reliable party, I don't know where he'd find one."

"What's this—remuner—remuner—whatever it is?" asked Weedly.

"Remuneration," said Freddy. "It's a fancy name for wages. My goodness, if I could live on somebody's big estate all summer and get paid for it at the same time . . . !" He jumped up. "I'm going into Centerboro to see Mr. Weezer. Want to come along?"

So the three animals went out the gate and down the road towards the village. In the excitement of a new idea Freddy had forgotten all about the heat, and he trotted along briskly, talking all the time about his plans for a summer which was evidently to be the most comfortable and luxurious summer spent by any pig that ever lived. "And you'll come to visit me," he said, "and we'll lie out in hammocks under the trees on the lawn and have ice cream and cakes and ginger ale brought to us on little trays, and—"

"Yeah?" said Jinx. "Who's going to carry the little trays?"

"H'm, that's so," said Freddy thoughtfully. "If the owner of this estate wants a caretaker, I suppose the house is closed, and all the servants will be gone. However," he said, brightening,

" 'remuneration generous'—remember? I'll be earning enough money to hire somebody to carry the little trays. Don't you worry, Jinx; you'll get your ice cream, all right."

"Wish I had some now," panted Weedly. "My goodness, Cousin Frederick, for anyone that complains about the heat you certainly burn up the road."

Freddy slowed down. "I'm sorry," he said. "We'll take a dip in the creek before we go into town. You don't want to go in to see a bank president all hot and sticky."

So it was a very cool-looking pair of pigs that was shown into Mr. Weezer's private office in the Centerboro Bank half an hour later. Jinx looked cool too, of course, although he hadn't gone swimming, for cats like hot weather.

Mr. Weezer was a small, thin, middle-aged man who wore very stiff white cuffs and a pair of nose glasses that always fell off when anyone mentioned a sum of money larger than five dollars. Of course, being in a bank, such sums were mentioned a hundred times a day, and so he wore his glasses on a black ribbon so that they wouldn't fall on the floor and break. Because these days even a bank president can't afford to buy new glasses every fifteen minutes or so.

To people who don't know Centerboro, it would seem surprising that a pig could be admitted to the office of the president of a bank. But the animals from the Bean farm were famous in that part of the state, and the Centerboro people were rather proud of them. Indeed, they received more invitations to dinners and parties in the village than they possibly could accept, for people thought no more of asking Freddy, or Jinx, or Hank, the old white horse, to stay to supper than you would of asking one of your own friends. And then of course as president of the first bank for animals ever opened in the United States, Freddy was a fellow member with Mr. Weezer of the State Bankers' Association.

"Well, well," said Mr. Weezer, getting up and shaking hands all around. "This is a pleasant surprise. And what can I do for you today? A little loan, perhaps?"

"No, thank you," said Freddy. "I came to enquire about this." And he showed Mr. Weezer the want ad.

Mr. Weezer read it, and then he leaned back in his chair and took off his glasses with one hand and tapped them on the fingers of the other hand and looked very serious as if he was considering

. . . a very cool-looking pair of pigs was shown into Mr. Weezer's private office.

thousands and thousands of dollars. "Ah, yes, I understand," he said.

Of course he didn't understand at all, and Freddy knew it. He knew that one of the first things a banker is taught to do is to look as important as possible during business hours, and always pretend to know just what the other fellow is thinking. Freddy could do that almost as well as Mr. Weezer could. But he was in a hurry to find out about the caretaker's job, and so he went right ahead and asked Mr. Weezer about it.

"Dear me," said Mr. Weezer. "This is rather unusual. It is unusual to have a pig apply for such a job, and it is unusual to have a bank president apply for it, but to have them both at once—" He shook his head thoughtfully. "I'm sure you would give satisfaction," he said, "and I'll be glad to recommend you for the job. But I don't know how Mr. Camphor will feel about hiring a pig."

"Is that Mr. C. Jimson Camphor?" Freddy asked.

"The same," said Mr. Weezer. He put on his glasses and picked up a pen and scribbled something on a card. "I suppose you know his estate?"

Freddy said he did. The Camphor estate was well known in all that part of the county. It was a big place on Otesaraga Lake, only a few miles north of the Bean farm. Mr. Camphor was a very rich man, and he had spared no expense in building himself a summer home. It was said that the house had forty rooms, and there were gardens and swimming pools and motor boats and tennis courts, and even a little outdoor theatre. Everything that Mr. Camphor had ever heard of that other rich men had, he immediately built. Freddy began to feel that he didn't have much chance of being selected to look after so magnificent a place.

Mr. Weezer handed Freddy the card. It was his personal calling card, and on the back he had written: "This will introduce my friend and colleague, Mr. Frederick Bean, President, First Animal Bank of Centerboro. I recommend him most highly. Anything you can do for him will be greatly appreciated. H. W."

"In ordinary times," said Mr. Weezer, "I don't think you'd have much chance of getting the job. But as you know, it is hard to find anyone for any kind of job nowadays. And I happen to know that Mr. Camphor, although he has advertised far and wide, has been unable to find anyone to take the position. It was as a last resort that he advertised in your paper. And may I suggest that you go to see him tomorrow? He's not home today, but he will be tomorrow, and I don't think you should lose any time."

Jinx, who so far had said nothing, now asked how much Mr. Camphor would pay.

"That I can't tell you," said Mr. Weezer. "But if you will take my advice, you will hold out for a good round sum." And as he said that, his glasses fell off.

The three animals dived at once for the spot on the marble floor where they thought the glasses would hit, with the result that their three noses came together with a painful scrunch. And the glasses, brought up short by the black ribbon, dangled unharmed above their heads.

After they had got up and their eyes had stopped watering, Mr. Weezer thanked them and said he hoped they hadn't hurt themselves, and Freddy thanked Mr. Weezer, and then they all shook hands and the animals left.

"I wonder how much old Camphor will really pay you?" Jinx said as they left the bank.

"Pooh," said Freddy, "I don't care if he doesn't pay me anything. If I can only get the job." Then he said thoughtfully: "But when Mr. Weezer spoke of a good round sum, his glasses fell off. So I'll ask at least five dollars."

Chapter 2

After he got back from Centerboro Freddy spent
the rest of the day and most of the evening getting the pigpen in order and putting out things
to take with him in case he really did get the caretaker job. He made a big pile of these things,
and then he went over them one by one, saying
to himself: "Now, do I really need this, or shall
I leave it here?" All this was a great waste of time,
for he couldn't make up his mind to do without
any of the things, and the pile was just as big

when he had gone over it as it had been when he started.

After that he made out a list. It looked like this:

THINGS TO DO BEFORE LEAVING

> Cover up typewriter
> See Mr. Bean
> Give going-away party (?)
> Close bank
> Collect 10¢ Robert owes me
> Get Mr. Bean's permission
> Show Weedly about being reporter
> Lock window
> Explain to Mr. Bean

The list was much longer, and writing it was a good deal of wasted time too, because he could have done many of the things in the time it took to write them down. But Freddy liked making lists of things. He had a feeling of satisfaction when he had written down something to do. It was almost as if he had really done it. And of course much less trouble.

He felt specially that way about getting Mr. Bean's permission to go away. That is why he had it on his list eight times. Mr. Bean was very fond of all his animals, and proud of them too, and he very seldom refused them anything they wanted. But he had a very gruff way of speaking which made them always a little afraid of him. My private opinion is that his gruffness was all put on, to hide the affection he really felt for the animals. Or it may have been just the way his voice came out through his whiskers. He had a very bushy beard which concealed almost his entire face, and even the kindest voice coming through such whiskers might well get changed into something else. I guess you would sound pretty gruff if you had to say everything through what was almost a small haystack.

Freddy went on adding things to his list and going through his belongings until at last about eleven o'clock he decided to go to bed. "My goodness," he said as he snapped out the light, "I suppose I might just as well sit up. I'm so excited that I shan't sleep a wink!" He put his head down on the pillow and closed his eyes and sighed, and then he sighed again, but halfway through the third sigh it turned into a snore, and he didn't know anything until Charles, the rooster, woke him up the next morning.

As soon as he put his nose outside the door he knew that it was going to be an even hotter day than yesterday, so after a hurried breakfast he started out to call on Mr. Camphor. It was nearly eight miles by road to Otesaraga Lake, but if you went up the brook and through the Bean woods, and then up through the Big Woods and over the hill, you came out in a wide valley. And if you crossed that valley and went over the next hill, there was the lake. That way it was only about three miles.

Freddy walked up along the brook. When he got to the duck pond, there were Jinx and Weedly, talking to Alice and Emma, the two ducks. Under a bush near them sat the ducks' Uncle Wesley, with his head under his wing.

"Hello, Freddy," said Jinx. "Weedly and I thought we'd take the day off and go up to the lake with you if you want us to."

"Glad to have company," said the pig. "What's the matter with Uncle Wesley?" he asked. "Isn't he going to get up this morning?" For it is unusual to see any animal or bird still sleeping after the rooster has crowed three times to get them all up.

"He isn't asleep," said Alice. "He's just meditating."

"About what?" Jinx asked.

"Oh, I don't know. He says the things Emma and I talk about aren't half as interesting as his own thoughts, and he sits that way so he can think and won't have to listen to our chatter."

"You mean he's not listening to us now?" asked Weedly, looking curiously at the sleeping duck.

"I'm sure he doesn't hear a thing we say," said Alice.

"Oh, yeah?" said Jinx. He winked at Freddy, then said in a loud voice: "Well, that's good, because there's something I wanted to tell you that I didn't want him to hear." Then he lowered his voice and said very fast under his breath: "Umbly, umbly, umbly, umbly."

And Uncle Wesley's head popped out from under his wing.

"Ah!" he said. "Company! Good morning Jinx, Weedly. Good morning, Freddy, my boy. Were you saying something, Jinx?"

"No," said the cat, pretending to look embarrassed. "No indeed, nothing important. Oh, no."

"Come, come," said the duck, waddling up to Jinx in his fussy pompous way, "no need to hide anything from Uncle Wesley. He can keep a secret, I imagine, as well as any of you, eh?"

"Well, if you really want to know what I was saying—" Jinx began, then paused.

"Yes, yes," said Uncle Wesley impatiently.

"I said: umbly, umbly, umbly, umbly."

Uncle Wesley puffed out his chest. "You said *what*?"

"Umbly, umbly, umbly, umbly," repeated Jinx. Then he grinned, and the two pigs grinned, and even Alice and Emma tittered a little.

Uncle Wesley was no fool and he saw that the joke was on him. He was pretty grumpy about it at first, but when Freddy had assured him that they wouldn't play jokes on him if they didn't like him, and when Jinx had slapped him on the back and called him "Wes, old pal," he stopped sulking and became much interested in Freddy's proposed call on Mr. Camphor. "I'd like to go along with you," he said, "but I guess it's pretty far. My feet, you know." He held up one yellow webbed foot for their inspection. "Aquatic sports, now; I'm your duck for that. But walking in the woods—no, no."

"If I get the position," said Freddy, "we'll have a picnic some day, and Hank can bring you up and we'll all go swimming in the lake." Then he turned to Jinx. "Well, come on; let's get started."

They went·on up the brook, and as they turned into the woods they looked back. Alice and Emma were swimming about peacefully, and Uncle Wesley, with his head under his wing, had returned to his meditations.

It was cool and damp in the woods; in many places it was so wet underfoot that the pigs splashed along ankle deep in water, and Jinx, who hated getting his feet wet, rode on Freddy's back. Here and there patches of unmelted snow still remained in hollows and under sheltered banks. After they had passed out of the Bean woods and across the back road into the Big Woods, the ground was drier, and Jinx trotted along ahead looking for squirrels. He liked to tease squirrels. He seldom chased them, but would sit on the ground and make faces at them, and the squirrels, who are rather short-tempered animals, would get madder and madder, chattering and screaming and jumping up and down until they almost fell off the branches. It was lots of fun.

But Jinx didn't see many squirrels in the Big Woods, for although the Ignormus had been exposed and defeated by Freddy and his friends, the animals were still a little fearful of the place where he had lived for so many years, and few of them cared to settle there. Even Freddy, remembering how scared he had been in the past among those big trees, hurried along a little faster, and he was glad when they were over the hill and came out into bright sunlight again on the farther slope.

They crossed the valley, climbed the long rise to the top of the next hill, and there before them stretched the blue waters of Otesaraga Lake, sparkling in the sun. And beside the lake stretched the green lawns of the Camphor estate, and they were almost as smooth as the water. Among the trees at the right they could see the roof of the big house.

Freddy stopped short. "My goodness," he said, "do you suppose the caretaker would have to keep all that lawn mowed?" He turned around. "Come on, let's go back."

"Hey, what's the matter with you, pig?" said Jinx. "You haven't come all this way to be scared out by a little lawn mowing, have you? Best exercise in the world. And goodness knows, you need it!" he said, poking Freddy in the side.

"I don't need it that much," said Freddy. "Look at the size of the place! Why, if you started with a lawn mower at this end and went around, the grass would have grown six inches high before you got back to it."

"Well, if you want to go home again, all right,"

said the cat. "Be quite an honor to have charge of such a grand place. You'd be a pretty important person around here. But of course if you don't think you're good enough to tackle the job, there's nothing more to say."

"Oh, well," said Freddy, "as long as we're here, I suppose I might as well go down and find out what there is to it. I don't have to take it if I don't want to."

"Certainly *not!*" said Jinx and Weedly together, and they winked at each other and followed Freddy down the hill.

Pretty soon they came to the high wall that surrounded the estate, and they followed this along till they found some iron gates. The gates were open and they went through them and up a long drive that wound in and out among trees and shrubbery until it came to the house. Freddy and Weedly hung back a little when they came in sight of the house, but Jinx went straight up the middle with his tail in the air as if he owned the place. But when they got to the front door he stood aside.

"O K, pig," he said. "Do your stuff."

So Freddy went up to the door. He didn't go very fast, but he went. And he rang the bell.

He waited about two seconds and then he

turned around. "Nobody home," he said. "Well, let's go." And he started down the steps.

But Jinx stopped him. "Give 'em time to answer, can't you?" he said. "My goodness, Freddy, what are you afraid of?"

"I'm not afraid exactly," said Freddy, "but— well, this is a lot bigger and grander house than I thought it would be. After all, I'm just a pig."

"It isn't as grand as the White House," said Jinx, "and when we went to Florida we all went there and shook hands with the President. I guess—"

He stopped, for the door opened slowly and a very tall dignified man in a black coat with tails stood in the doorway. He was so dignified that he didn't even lower his eyes to see who had rung the bell, but just looked straight out about two feet over Freddy's head. And so he did not see that Freddy was a pig.

"I am—is Mr. Camphor home?" Freddy asked.

"Who shall I say wishes to see him?" the man inquired, still looking off into the distance.

"Mr. Frederick Bean," said Freddy, who was beginning to gain confidence. "And friends," he added.

The man stood aside. "Pray step in," he said. "I will see if Mr. Camphor is at home."

"Pray, step in," he said.

The three animals filed past him into the hall, and as he closed the door behind them, Freddy held out the card that Mr. Weezer had given him. "Will you please give Mr. Camphor this?" he said.

The man had to bend down to take the card, and then he saw them. He gave a sharp bark of surprise. "Pigs!" he exclaimed. "Oh, my aunt— pigs!" He stared for a moment, then turned suddenly and wrenched at the door. "Outside!" he gabbled. "Out with you! Shoo! Scat!" Then he gave a yell, for in stepping back as he pulled the door open, he had trod on Jinx's tail, and the cat had clawed him sharply in the leg.

The animals were scrambling for the door when a voice called "Stop!" and they looked around to see a short red-faced man with a moustache who had come into the hall through a door at the back. "What's going on here? Shut that door, Bannister."

The tall man closed the door. "These animals, sir," he said. "I give you my word, sir, they rang the bell and asked for you. If you'll pardon my saying so, sir, I never heard of such a thing in all me life."

"Certainly I will pardon you," said the man, "but I don't think that the remark is very interesting. What's that in your hand?" And he came forward and took the card and read it. "First Animal Bank, eh? Of course, I remember seeing the sign. 'Assets: none; liabilities: unlimited,' or something of the kind, eh?"

"No, sir," said Freddy, "it's the other way round."

"Ah," said the man. "Well, one never knows with banks, does one?" He smiled pleasantly at Freddy, then turned to the butler. "Bannister, you're a fool."

"Yes, Mr. Camphor," said the man, but he didn't look as if he minded much.

"You are getting old."

"As you say, sir."

"And, Bannister, there's no fool like an old fool."

"I don't know that I agree with you there, sir," said Bannister seriously.

"Ah," said Mr. Camphor, "that's an interesting question. Perhaps you're right. You believe that a young fool looks foolisher than an old fool, do you? What's your opinion, Mr. Bean?"

"Oh, please just call me Freddy," said the pig.

"Glad to; glad to," said Mr. Camphor. "You may call me Jimson if you like. I'm not one to stand on ceremony. Never had much dignity. That's why I keep Bannister, here. He has to be dignified for two of us." He looked at the other animals. "Your friends, Mr.—ah, Freddy?"

Freddy introduced them, and Mr. Camphor shook hands with them, while Bannister stood stiffly, looking over their heads without any expression at all.

"Well," said Mr. Camphor, "what are we standing here for? Bannister, some—ha, some refreshments on the north terrace. Come with me, gentlemen."

He led the way through a series of elegantly furnished rooms and out a long window on to a shady terrace which faced across the lake.

"Make yourselves comfortable. Jinx, you take that chair with the cushion. Now, gentlemen, is this a—ha, a business conference or just a neighborly call?"

"I came to see you on business," said Freddy.

"Ha, I was afraid of that." Mr. Camphor looked unhappy. "Nobody ever pays just friendly calls on rich men. And I am a very rich man, gentlemen. That's the trouble with having a lot of money—nobody ever comes just to see *me*. They always want to sell me something, or get me to give money to something, or—or something. Always something to do with money, at any rate. Never just friendly talk about the weather, and politics, and—and food." He shook his head. "Money is the root of all evil."

"I don't agree with you, sir," said Bannister, appearing with a large tray.

"Eh? You don't?" Mr. Camphor swung around and looked at the man, who had set the tray down and was placing a large saucer of cream before Jinx. "Dear me, that's two proverbs in one day that we have disagreed on."

"I don't think you believe it either, sir," said Bannister. "If you did, you'd give all your money away, wouldn't you, sir?"

"Ha, by George, I believe you're right," said Mr. Camphor. "Wouldn't want to keep the root of all evil right in my pocket, would I? Well, Freddy, as a banker, what do you say to that?— Here, try some of these little cakes."

"I don't know," said Freddy. "The money in our bank isn't a lot of trouble, but of course there isn't very much of it. But anyway, Mr. Camph—"

"Jimson to you, remember," interrupted Mr. Camphor. "Though if this is a business conference, perhaps we'd better stick to the misters." Then he smiled at Freddy. "No, no; you stick to Jimson."

"Well, sir," said Freddy, "—I mean Jimson; I was just going to say that while I came on business, my friends just came along to—well, to pay a call."

"You wouldn't say that they came out of curiosity?" asked Mr. Camphor.

"Yes, sir—Jimson, of course they did. But there's no harm in that, is there?"

"None—ha, none at all," agreed Mr. Camphor. "But that brings up another proverb: curiosity killed the cat. What do you say to that, Bannister?"

"I don't believe it, sir. This cat, if I may say so, is almost too much alive."

"I'm sorry I clawed you," said Jinx. "But when you stepped on my tail—"

"Pray don't mention it, sir," said Bannister. "I should no doubt have clawed you if you'd done the same thing to me."

"Well, well," said Mr. Camphor, "let's get the business part of this meeting over, and then we can get to the gossip and refreshments. What did you want to see me about, Freddy? —Bannister, kindly provide dignity for a business conference."

So Bannister stood up very stiff, with his elbows well away from his sides, and Freddy told

Mr. Camphor about seeing the advertisement, and about wanting to apply for the job of caretaker.

"Dear me," said Mr. Camphor when he had finished. "It's hard to tell whether you'd be suitable or not. It's rather buying a pig in a poke, isn't it? Not that I ever knew what a poke was, and in any case I don't think you're in one, so we'd better let that proverb go. But I've never employed a pig before." He looked at Freddy thoughtfully. "On the other hand, I've never employed a bank president. A bank president as caretaker—ha, that sounds rather fine, doesn't it? H'm, well . . . Of course, nobody else has applied for the job—you know how hard it is to get help nowadays. But perhaps I'd better tell you just what the work is." He leaned back in his chair and lit a large cigar. "I shall be in Washington all summer working for the government, but I shall come up occasionally for the weekend, so the house will not be closed. Mrs. Winch, my cook, will keep it open, and have a room always ready for me. She will also cook the meals for the caretaker.

"The caretaker's duties are quite simple," he went on. "He will be a sort of policeman. He will guard the house and the grounds. In case

of boys and wild animals, he will be expected
to drive them away. In case of burglars, he will
be expected to—ha, to capture them. But as I
understand from Mr. Weezer that you are a
competent detective, and in addition, a good
friend of the sheriff's, I think you would be able
to manage that."

"Yes, sir—Jimson. I think so," said Freddy
doubtfully. "Where does the—the caretaker
live?"

Mr. Camphor got up. "Come to the edge of
the terrace," he said. "You see down there,
where the creek comes into the lake?"

"That little house?" said Freddy.

"Yes, it's a houseboat. Has three little rooms,
completely furnished. There's an outboard
motor attached to it, so that you can cruise
around the lake if you want to, and tie up for
the night wherever you happen to be. It doesn't
go very fast, of course. And I wouldn't expect
the caretaker to go off on a long cruise and leave
the estate unattended."

"A houseboat!" exclaimed Freddy. "Oh, my
goodness, Mr.—Jimson, I hope you will give me
the job. I'd love to spend a summer on a houseboat."

"Well," said Mr. Camphor thoughtfully, "I

think perhaps I will. Mr. Weezer spoke very highly of you. And—oh yes, the pay. The caretaker gets fifty dollars a month and the houseboat and all his meals. I trust that would be satisfactory?"

"Satisfactory!" Freddy exclaimed. "Why it's —it's too much! My goodness, what would I do with all that money?"

"Ha! Hear that, Bannister?" said Mr. Camphor. "Only person I ever hired who was satisfied with my first offer. The workman is worthy of his hire—ha, there's a proverb we can try out. We'll see if you're worthy of your hire, Freddy. And by the way, I understand you're something of a writer? Write poetry, eh?"

"Why, I—I dabble in it a little, sir," said Freddy modestly.

"Good! Good! You'll have plenty of time for dabbling. But what I wanted to suggest— As you may have noticed, I'm much interested in proverbs. You know what I mean: such things as 'a rolling stone gathers no moss.' Well, most people accept these proverbs as true. But Bannister and I don't agree with 'em. Ha! I guess we don't. We argue about them, and when we can we try them out, to prove whether they're really true or not. That rolling stone one, for instance. We rolled hundreds of stones down that hill over there. Well, some of them *did* gather moss. Not much, but enough to prove that the proverb isn't always true. If we rolled 'em down where there was plenty of moss, they picked up a little on the way.

"Well, what I wanted to say was this. If in your spare time you can examine into a few proverbs, why I'll pay you a little extra. For every proverb you experiment with, ten dollars. How's that? You see, Bannister and I expect to write a book about them when we gather enough facts. But we need help. And I think perhaps you're just the person to help us. What do you say?"

Of course Freddy was delighted with the idea and said so.

"Fine!" said Mr. Camphor. "Splendid! Well then, that's all settled. Report for duty a week from today. And now that business is over, there's no more need for dignity. Relax, Bannister. Sit down and have a cake."

Chapter 3

One evening two weeks later Freddy lay comfortably stretched out in a canvas chair under the blue and white striped awning on the deck of the houseboat. After the warm day when he had paid his first visit to the Camphor estate it had turned cold, but now after two days of rain it was again warm enough to sit outdoors. Freddy looked out across the darkening water to where lights on the farther shore, a mile away, were beginning to twinkle, and he listened to the peaceful lap-lap of the little waves against the houseboat's hull, and he thought: "Golly, I'm a lucky pig!"

And of course he was. His job was a pretty pleasant one. Every morning he went up to the house and Mrs. Winch gave him his breakfast. Then he spent about an hour walking around the estate and inspecting everything to see that nothing had gone wrong during the night. Then he went back to the houseboat and rested until Mrs. Winch had his lunch ready. After lunch he inspected the house to see that everything was in order, and after another walk around the estate he rested until dinnertime. Then, just before going to bed, he went down and locked the big iron gates.

Today he had mowed the lawn for the first time. It wasn't nearly as much of a job as he had been afraid it would be, for there was a gasoline lawn mower. Mr. Camphor had showed him how to run it, and all he had to do was sit in the seat and steer, and the little knives whirred under him as he drove along and sent up the cut grass blades in a green spray behind him. He had gone straight up and down at first, but when he got tired of that, he steered in curves and circles, and made patterns so that the lawn looked like a huge green figured carpet. Of course he couldn't leave it that way and he had to go around and cut all the rest of it afterwards, but it was lots of fun.

The only unpleasant part of his job was Mrs. Winch. She didn't like animals, and she specially didn't like pigs. When asked why, she merely said: "A pig is a pig; that's reason enough, I should think." There isn't much you can do with a person like that.

Mrs. Winch was a small, thin, elderly woman with a sort of vinegary expression. She was a hard worker and a fine cook, but it was no use trying to get on the right side of her by praising her cooking. When Freddy told her the first night that it was a good dinner, she just said: "Of course it's a good dinner. Why shouldn't it be?" And when he went on to say that it was the best dinner he had ever had, she replied crossly: "I should think it very likely. It would be news to me that any pig was a judge of good cooking." Fortunately, she was one of those cooks who are so proud of their skill that they can't bear to put a meal on the table that isn't as good as they can make it. If she hadn't been, she would have liked to serve Freddy poor meals. Later on, she did try to find out if there were any dishes which he specially disliked. But Freddy was too clever for her there. He was extremely fond of strawberry shortcake, but he told her he didn't like it very well. So twice a day as long as the strawberry season lasted he had shortcake.

After the sun had gone the air grew cool, and Freddy got up and walked down the drive to the gates and locked them for the night. Then he came back to the houseboat. He went into the little living room and lit the lamp and sat down in one of the armchairs. He was getting sleepy, but he hated to go to bed. It was such a nice little living room. It wasn't much bigger than his study at home, but it was much more elegantly furnished. There were two armchairs with chintz slip covers on them, and at the four little windows there were curtains that matched the covers. In the middle of the room, under the big hanging lamp, was a table, and on it were writing materials, and a portable radio, and a photograph album. Against one wall was a bookcase containing perhaps fifty brand new detective stories, and against the opposite wall another case containing more serious works. In one corner stood an easel with a large crayon drawing of Mr. Camphor propped up on it.

All around the room close to the ceiling hung framed photographs of famous places like Niagara Falls and the Roman Forum and the church of Notre Dame in Paris. Sometimes it was hard to see the famous places, because they were also photographs of Mr. Camphor, who seemed to have always stepped in front of the camera just before the photographer clicked the shutter. So that they were really pictures of Mr. Camphor with Niagara Falls in the background, and of Mr. Camphor in front of Notre Dame, and of Mr. Camphor against the Roman Forum. But Freddy didn't mind that, because he liked Mr. Camphor.

After a while Freddy got up and opened the door to the bedroom and looked in. It certainly was a snug little bedroom, and the white pillow and the peach-colored down quilt looked very inviting. It was nice to sit up, all right, with the little curtains drawn over the windows and the warm lamplight falling full upon the pages of some absorbing story. But after all . . . Freddy yawned. And then he reached up to turn out the light. And as he did so there was a faint scuffling noise outside the door, and then a very light tap.

At first he thought it was just the water lapping the hull of the houseboat, but then it came again. He went to the door and opened it. Two large hoptoads squatted side by side on the threshold.

They blinked their bulging eyes in the light, and one of them said: "Are you the new care-taker?"

"Yes," said Freddy. "What can I do for you?"

"Maybe you can do something and maybe you can't," said the toad. "My name is Elmo, and this is my brother, Waldo."

"Well, step in, step in," said Freddy hospi-tably, and he bent down and shook their clammy little paws. "Very happy to make your acquaint-ance. And I'll be glad to do anything I can."

They hopped in. "Nice little place you've got here," said Elmo, looking around.

"If you care for this sort of thing," said Waldo.

"Yes," said Freddy. "I do, you see. Can I offer you some refreshment?"

"Got any mosquitoes?" Elmo asked.

"I'm afraid not," Freddy said. "These screens on the windows keep them out."

"Poor sort of place with no mosquitoes," re-marked Waldo.

"I could make you a cup of cocoa," said

Freddy, who, since he was taking all his meals at the house, had not yet had a chance to try out the resources of the well-stocked little kitchen.

"Oh, no thanks," said Elmo, and Waldo shuddered.

"Well," said Freddy, "I'd like to entertain you. You're the first callers I've had in my new home. But if you don't like cocoa . . . H'm. Would you like me to read you some of my poetry?"

"That would be very nice," said Elmo, "but—"

"Speak for yourself," grunted Waldo.

"—but perhaps," Elmo went on, "we'd better tell you why we came. You see, this Mr. Camphor, he's a very nice man. He's very kind to all the animals on his estate. He puts out food for them, and he never throws stones at them or shoots guns at them or anything."

"He don't like hoptoads," put in Waldo.

"I don't think he dislikes us," said Elmo, "but he's afraid of us. He thinks we'd give him warts if he petted us. But I don't suppose you could change the way he feels about that."

"Perhaps I could," said Freddy. "Was that what you wanted me to do?"

"It would be nice if you could," said Elmo,

"but that wasn't really why we came. We wanted to do him a good turn. You see there are some rats living in the attic of the big house. He doesn't know about it, because Mrs. Winch hasn't told him. She thinks that if he knew, he'd want her to get a cat, and she doesn't like cats. She sets traps, but they're too smart to be caught. They just spring them with a stick and then eat the bait."

"Yes, they're smart, all right," said Freddy. "I suppose they steal a lot of food too."

"I don't think that matters so much," said Elmo. "Mr. Camphor is a rich man, and I guess the little they eat wouldn't cramp him. But they are destroying a lot of nice things up there. All his family portraits, for one thing. They chew holes in them."

"How do you happen to know about this?" Freddy asked.

"We've been up there," said Elmo. "Would you care to go up and look for yourself?"

"If you ain't afraid," said Waldo.

Freddy was pretty curious to know how a hoptoad could get into the house and even up into the attic, so he said yes, he certainly would.

"Come along, then," said Elmo, and the two toads hopped towards the door. Freddy took a flashlight and followed them. They hopped along the gangway that made a bridge from the houseboat to the bank of the creek, and then upstream a little way until they came to a thick clump of bushes that grew close to the water against the highest part of the bank. Then they hopped right into the bushes and disappeared.

Freddy hesitated a minute, then pushed through after them. In the beam of the flashlight he saw them hopping ahead of him along a narrow passageway roofed over with planks, which were supported by a plank wall reinforced every few feet with heavy beams.

"Hey," said Freddy, "what is this—a secret passage?"

"Yes," said Elmo. "Mr. Camphor built it when he built the house. He'd seen secret passages in some old castles in Europe, and he thought it would be fun to have one himself. It's really secret, too, because even Mrs. Winch doesn't know about it. We found it last summer when we were looking for a nice damp dark place to live. And then later we explored it. That's how we found out about the rats. Come on; we'll show you."

Hoptoads can travel pretty fast when they want to. They hopped along at a good clip, and pretty soon the passage began to go uphill a little. Then it leveled out again and they went through a stone arch, and Elmo said they were in the cellar.

"It's a funny thing about rats," Elmo said. "If they just took food you could understand it. But they seem to like to tear up things just for the fun of destroying them. Have you had much experience with them?"

"Have I!" Freddy exclaimed. "Say, the things I could tell you about rats would make your hair curl." Then he laughed. "Only of course hoptoads don't have any hair, do they?"

"Don't get personal," Waldo snapped.

"Say, what are you so grumpy about?" Freddy demanded. "I'm doing what you want me to, aren't I?"

"Don't mind Waldo," said Elmo. "He's just contrary. He doesn't mean anything by it. Mother tried and tried to teach him not to contradict, but she couldn't break him of it. Look, Freddy, here are the stairs. They go up in the thickness of the wall. We'd better not talk any more. We don't want Mrs. Winch to hear."

Halfway up the first flight was a landing, and Elmo whispered to Freddy that there were peepholes through the wall on both sides. "They're too high for us to get up to," he said, "so I don't know what rooms you can see."

Freddy thought he could see a faint beam of light on one side, but it came through the wall a good foot above his head. They went up a second flight, which was also broken by a landing, and on this landing was a door which Elmo said opened into Mr. Camphor's bedroom. "At least it snored like Mr. Camphor," he said.

The second flight ended at the top in a door, which stood ajar. Freddy had been wondering how the toads had got into the attic, and now he saw that it was because the door hadn't been closed. For if there is one thing a hoptoad can't do it is open a closed door.

The toads hopped through and Freddy followed, pushing through a lot of old suits and overcoats that were hung on the other side of the door to conceal it. And there they were in the attic.

It was an enormous attic, crowded with trunks and boxes and old furniture and odds and ends of every kind. In fact it was just like everybody else's attic, only larger.

The toads hopped off in a far corner. "Here," said Elmo, "look at this."

Freddy turned his flashlight on a row of large

pictures in heavy gilded frames that stood against the wall. They were portraits of men and women in old-fashioned costumes—wigs and ruffs and satin coats and even one or two in armor, and they certainly were badly chewed. There was a little brass plate on each portrait, with the name of the subject. Freddy read them. Sir George Camphor. The Right Reverend Wilberforce Camphor. Lady Elizabeth Camphor. His Eminence, Cardinal Camphor. And there were two little boys in black satin suits, with long curls, who were Lord Percy, and the Right Honorable Fitzhugh Camphor.

There were holes in nearly all the canvases. "My goodness," said Freddy, "what a distinguished family Mr. Camphor comes from! That was pretty mean of the rats. Look at Sir George; he hasn't any face left. And the Right Reverend Wilberforce has had his wig chewed off. I'll bet Mr. Camphor will be hopping mad when he sees this."

A faint snicker interrupted him. He swung the flashlight around, and in the darkness under a big wardrobe two yellow sparks glittered.

"Come out of there," he said sternly. "Come out and let's see you."

Both toads hopped closer to the pig as an old

grey rat came out from under the wardrobe. He twitched his whiskers and grinned wickedly at Freddy. "Well, well," he said in an oily voice, "fancy meeting you here, pig! What a small place the world is, to be sure. Well, don't you recognize me? Haven't you a warm handshake for your old friend, Simon?"

"No, I haven't got a handshake for you, Simon," said Freddy severely. "But I've got a neckshake for you if you're making any trouble, and it certainly looks as if you were." It worried Freddy to find Simon and his family here. For they were not just ordinary rats. Twice in the past they had caused serious trouble at the Bean farm, and it had taken all Freddy's cleverness and the help of most of the other animals to drive them away.

"Dear, dear," said Simon, shivering in mock alarm, "what a ferocious pig! And who are these two warty gentlemen?" he asked, his slanting eyes darting a look at the toads. "Your bodyguard, I presume. Tut, tut; such tough, sturdy fellows! I expect I'll just have to surrender. What chance would a feeble old fellow like me have against such a display of force?"

Freddy would have had no hesitation in attacking Simon, but he knew that the old rat was

not alone. Zeke and Ezra, and all the other sons
and grandsons would be lurking in the dark
corners of the attic, and he was sure that at the
first show of violence the whole crew would
pitch into him. He wouldn't have a chance.

"Look here, Simon," he said, "I don't bear
you any ill will. But I'm caretaker of this place
now. If you wanted to live here quietly, I don't
know that I'd try to drive you away. But this
destruction of property is something else again.
It's got to stop. Why, look at those beautiful
pictures! Why did you have to spoil them? They
aren't good to eat. And what will Mr. Camphor
say when he finds out that you ruined all the
portraits of his ancestors, and I didn't do anything to stop you?"

"His ancestors! Ha, that's a good one!"
Simon giggled, and his giggle was echoed by
snickers from other parts of the attic. "You
don't suppose those are his real ancestors, do
you? Dear me, you're very simple, even for a
pig. They're just a lot of old pictures he bought
up different places; nobody knows who they
were, least of all your great Mr. Camphor. And
as to why we chewed 'em up—well, we just got
sick of seeing the things around. Us rats have
got artistic souls, pig. If they were good paint-

ings, we wouldn't touch 'em; we'd sit around and oh and ah over 'em all day. But they're pretty bad jobs of painting. Why, turn your light on Lord Montague Camphor, there," he said, pointing to the picture of a languid young man in blue satin who was leaning against a broken pillar. "Look at that nose. Ever see such rotten painting in your life? It probably doesn't look any more like the person it was painted from than you look like General MacArthur. Why, it's our artistic duty to chew 'em up."

Freddy had to admit that the painting was pretty terrible. "But Mr. Camphor likes it," he said, "and it's his property. You've no right to touch it."

"Listen, Freddy," said Simon, becoming serious for a moment. "We rats don't bear any grudge against you. You gave us a break the last time we left the Bean farm, and in return we promised never to come back and bother you again. But you can't chase all over the country, driving us out of every home we settle in. It isn't fair. Now you just be a good pig and leave us alone, and we'll leave you alone. Eh? How about it?"

"And suppose I don't?" said Freddy.

"Ah, that would be just too bad. Too bad for

you, and for—" he snarled suddenly at the toads
"—those two tattletales!" The toads hopped
right under Freddy. "Yes," Simon went on,
"peekers and priers and sneaky snoops; we rats
know how to get rid of such people."

"Yah! Is that so!" Waldo yelled from under
Freddy. "We aren't afraid of you!"

"My, my!" said Simon, grinning; "such a
brave toad! And quite right, too. Why should
anybody be afraid of kind old Simon? Come out,
toad, and let poor old Simon pat you on the
head."

"Keep still, rat," said Freddy. "And you too,
Waldo. You and Elmo go on down the passage;
I'll be along in a minute." And when the toads
had done as he told them, he said: "I'm giving
you warning, Simon. If you and your gang want
to live here quietly, all right. But if you're going to destroy Mr. Camphor's property, I'll
have to take measures."

"Take the measure of your own tombstone,
pig, if you plan to interfere with us," said the
rat.

Freddy didn't answer. He went over and began pulling one of the smaller portraits towards
the door. It was a picture of Sir Archibald
Camphor, a knight in full armor. The vizor of

his helmet was up, but where the face should have been there was just a hole where the rats had gnawed away the canvas.

Simon didn't try to stop him. He sat back and watched, chuckling to himself. "What you going to do, pig? Get an ancestor or two for yourself? Let me congratulate you; you have made an excellent choice. I see a marked family resemblance to you in this Sir Archibald's face. The same soulful expression, the same delicately chiseled features." He snickered. " 'Chiseled' is good! And here are the chisels that chiseled 'em." He showed his long yellow teeth.

But Freddy paid him no further attention. He dragged the picture out and down the stairs, then lugged it through the secret passage to the houseboat. The toads followed him, and when they were back in Freddy's living room, Elmo said:

"Well, I think we did the right thing by taking you up there, but I'm afraid it will get us into trouble. That rat was pretty mad at us. We won't dare live in the passage any more."

"I don't think he'll bother you," said Freddy. "But you can come live here with me if it would make you feel safer."

But Elmo didn't want to do that. Toads don't

care much for elegant surroundings. What they like best is a good damp cellar with lots of bugs.

"Well," said Freddy, "why don't you move into that pile of rocks just beyond the entrance to the secret passage? It's damp, and close to the water, and it's certainly as buggy a place as anybody could wish."

"I guess we'll have to," said Elmo. "I'll be sorry to move, though. We have been very happy there."

Freddy said he didn't see why they were so attached to the place. After all, it was just a hole under a rock.

"It may be just a hole under a rock to you, but to us it is our home," said Elmo simply.

"Yeah," said Waldo, "and now we've got to move, all on account of you."

"If it's on account of anything, it's on account of the rats," said Freddy.

"Yes," said Elmo. "It's not Freddy's fault."

" 'Tis too!" said Waldo. "Why didn't he drive 'em away? That's what we took him up there for. And all he did was just stand there and let that old Simon tell him where he got off."

"Look, Waldo," said Freddy; "I could lick Simon in a fight all right. But I've only got one set of teeth to fight with, and Simon has a dozen —all his sons and nephews and nieces and cousins. And while I was chewing him up, what would they be doing? There are better ways of getting rid of them than for me to try to throw them out."

"Yeah?" sneered Waldo. "What are they?"

"I've got to think about it," said Freddy. "I haven't any plan yet."

"Yeah, and while you're talking, the rats chew us up."

"Well, I wouldn't much care if they did chew you up, Waldo," said Freddy crossly. "My goodness, I thought hoptoads prided themselves on their good manners, but you seem to be proud of having bad ones."

"I am not!" said Waldo. "I've got just as good manners as you have."

"All right, all right," said Freddy wearily. "I'm not going to argue with you about everything I say. I'm tired and I want to go to bed. Now Elmo, you two better move into those rocks for a few days. As soon as I have a plan I'll let you know about it."

When Elmo had apologized for Waldo, and Waldo had again contradicted him, the toads left. Freddy took the crayon drawing of Mr.

Camphor off the easel and propped up the painting of Sir Archibald Camphor in its place. Then he gave a terrible big yawn and turned out the light and went into the bedroom and climbed into bed and pulled the peach-colored down quilt up under his chin and went to sleep.

The next morning after he had made his tour of the estate, he went back to the houseboat and got out his palette and his brushes and his tubes of oil paint. For it had occurred to him that it would be a nice thing to fix up the portraits that the rats had chewed, so that Mr. Camphor would still have his ancestors. He put on a smock and a black satin beret such as artists sometimes wear, and he squeezed out some colors on the palette, and then he stood in front of the picture. He stooped and peered at it, and then he moved back a ways and regarded it with his head on one side. "Ah!" he said, and made sweeping motions with his brush. Then he turned the portrait upside down and did the same things over again.

All this was a sort of warming up, before he got really down to painting. It didn't mean anything. At least, Freddy didn't think it did, but he had seen a real artist once, painting a land-

"Ah," he said, and made sweeping motions with the brush.

scape with a bridge in it, who had gone through the same sort of performance, and he thought maybe it was the thing to do. Anyway, half the fun of painting is to look like an artist. That was why he had put on the beret and the smock.

After he had gone through these artistic motions for a while, he decided he had better get to work. So he dipped his brush in some color and stepped up to the canvas. Then he stopped. "My goodness," he said, "I forgot! There isn't anything to paint on! You can't paint a face on a hole. I'll have to glue a piece of canvas on the back, over the hole, before I can do anything."

He was just cutting a patch out of the roll of canvas he had brought with him when he heard voices, and looking out the window, saw all the animals from the Bean farm coming down the path toward the houseboat.

They were all there: Jinx and Weedly, Hank, the old white horse, Alice, Emma and Uncle Wesley, Robert and Georgie, the two dogs, Charles, the rooster, and Henrietta his wife, and the three cows, Mrs. Wiggins, Mrs. Wurzburger and Mrs. Wogus. Each cow had a large market basket hooked over one of her horns, and from the look of the baskets, which were covered with clean white napkins, Freddy knew it was a picnic. They had come over to have a picnic with him.

He started to go out, then he hesitated. After a moment's thought he giggled and, running to the door, opened it about halfway. Then he dashed back to the easel, pulled it around to face the door, and stepping behind it, shoved his head through the hole where Sir Archibald's face had been. He giggled again, then composed his features in as noble and warlike an expression as a pig is capable of, and waited expectantly.

Chapter 4

He heard footsteps on the gravel path, then thumping and scrabbling as they came aboard the houseboat, and a second or two later Mrs. Wurzburger's broad nose appeared in the doorway. She blinked at everything in an interested way but didn't seem to see the portrait. "Nobody home, I guess," she said over her shoulder. "Well, girls, put those baskets down in the shade and come on in. Guess he won't mind if we look around a little."

So the animals—or as many of them as could at one time—piled into the living room. Of course there wasn't room for three cows and a horse, besides all the smaller animals, so the larger ones poked their heads through the windows. They were all curious to see what kind of a place Freddy had got, and they looked into the bedroom and bounced on the bed to see if he had a soft mattress, and exclaimed over all the fine furnishings, and Hank, when he came in, even tried one of the armchairs, but when it gave a protesting creak he got up again.

"Well, my land," said Mrs. Wiggins, "Freddy's certainly living in the lap of luxury, isn't he?"

"Too fancy for my taste," said Hank. "Though, I dunno; maybe you get used to it."

"Hey, look," said Georgie, the little brown dog. "Freddy's had his paints out. Do you suppose he painted that picture there on the easel?"

The animals all gathered in front of the portrait. Freddy held perfectly still and tried not to wink.

"My, it's a nice picture!" said Mrs. Wogus. "What is it supposed to be?"

"It's a knight in full armor, silly," said Jinx.

"Freddy's always reading those stories about the Knights of the Round Table. Probably he thought he'd paint one."

"I bet none of those old knights ever had a nose like that," said Georgie. "It seems to stick right out of the picture."

"Of course it does," said Henrietta impatiently. "What's the matter with you animals—are you blind? It sticks out because it's a pig's nose. It isn't a knight in armor, it's a pig in armor. It's Freddy."

"Why it is, at that," said the animals. "He's painted himself as a Knight of the Round Table. Sir Freddy wins the prize at the tournament." And they all began to laugh.

But after they had laughed for a while, Mrs. Wiggins said: "I'm not so sure it's a picture of Freddy. He's a lot nicer looking than that."

"I think it's a picture of a camel," said Georgie.

"Well, if he did mean it for himself, he certainly didn't flatter himself any," said Jinx. "He looks sort of crosseyed."

"He's given himself a mean look, all right," said Robert, the collie. "And he looks so scrubby. Why, I wouldn't trust that pig around the corner of the barn."

"He's certainly the homeliest pig I ever saw, in armor or out," said Mrs. Wiggins. "I bet the other knights all got up and left the table."

This was too much for Freddy. "Oh, is that so?" he exclaimed, and he pulled his head out of the canvas and came around in front of the easel. "Homely, am I? Scrubby and cross-eyed, am I? A nice bunch of friends you are, calling me a lot of names as soon as my back is turned!"

The animals had jumped and edged away towards the door, but Jinx said: "Your back wasn't turned, pig. Everything that was said, we said right to your face, and you can't deny it."

"Aw, we knew it was you all the time, Freddy," said Georgie, and the others chimed in and agreed with him.

"Anyway," said Jinx, "when you stuck your head through that canvas, you really stuck your neck out, didn't you? You know, listeners never hear any good of themselves."

Freddy was still pretty mad, but Jinx's remark caught his attention. "What's that you said?"

"It's an old proverb," Jinx said. "Listeners never hear good of themselves."

"My goodness," said Freddy, "that one is true all right. I must save that one for Mr. Camphor."

"What on earth are you talking about?" said Mrs. Wiggins. So Freddy told her about Mr. Camphor's interest in proving whether the old proverbs and sayings were really true or not. "I get ten dollars extra for every one I experiment with," he explained. "Excuse me while I make a note of this one." And he went over to the table and jotted it down on a piece of paper. He had forgotten all about being mad.

The animals were interested in the proverb idea, and they thought up some for Freddy to experiment with. They thought of "All's well that ends well," and "The more haste the less speed," and "Better late than never," and then Jinx suggested "Seeing is believing." And he said: "I guess we've just been experimenting with that one."

"We certainly have," said Freddy. "And I guess it isn't true because you saw me, but you didn't believe it was me, now did you?"

"Sure we did. We knew you all the time," said Robert.

"Oh, come on, now," Freddy protested. "You don't have to pretend any more. I don't mind

This was too much for Freddy.

the things you said. My goodness, I know I'm not handsome."

"Handsome is as handsome does," said Mrs. Wiggins.

"Oh, golly!" Freddy exclaimed. "There's a good one! But I'm not sure I know just what it means."

"Why, I think it means, Freddy," said the cow, "that we don't care whether or not you're handsome to look at, because you do things in such a handsome way, and so you seem handsome to us."

"My gracious, that's a pretty nice compliment," said Freddy, and the tips of his ears got quite pink. But the animals all agreed that this was so, though there was some discussion as to just how handsome Freddy really was to look at. Jinx said that for a pig he was handsome enough, but in comparison to almost any cat he was no great shakes. Mrs. Wiggins said that in comparison to cows she thought him very well-favored indeed, though of course that wasn't saying much. And she laughed her great booming laugh that made the houseboat rock at its moorings. The argument was all in fun, but it rather scandalized the two ducks, who were never quick to see a joke.

"I must say," Alice remarked, "that this conversation seems to be in very bad taste. Discussing Freddy right to his face! I think, sister," she said, turning to Emma, "that we can best express our disapproval by stepping outside." And they waddled with dignity to the door.

So Freddy followed them out and explained, and then he took the animals on a tour of the estate, and after that they all came back and the baskets were opened and sandwiches and stuffed eggs and cakes and pickles and pies and bottles of pop were brought out, and they picnicked under the awning on the roof of the houseboat, which was flat and had a railing around it, so that it was almost like another porch.

While they were eating, Freddy told them about Simon and his gang. They were much concerned, but none of their suggestions for getting rid of the rats were very practical. Jinx was all for going up in the attic and fighting them, but as Freddy pointed out, they wouldn't fight—they'd just disappear down their holes and wait until Jinx had gone. Georgie suggested that they build a big fire in the attic and smoke the rats out. "And burn the house down," said Freddy. "That's a dandy idea!"

"Freddy," said Emma, "I hesitate to make a

suggestion—you're all so clever and resourceful, but if you were just to go up and talk to them nicely—just tell them that Mr. Camphor didn't like having them there, and ask them politely to leave . . . well, they wouldn't like to stay on where they're not wanted, would they?"

Most of the animals laughed, and Jinx said: "Gosh, Emma, you slay me!" But Freddy said no, he was afraid it wouldn't work. "I guess you haven't had much experience with rats, Emma," he said. "The only places they like to live are places where they aren't wanted. No, that wouldn't do. But don't you animals bother. I'll think of something before long. But let's not talk about unpleasant things. How are things going on the farm?"

So they told him all the gossip of the barn-yard, and then after lunch they cast off the ropes with which the houseboat was moored to the shore, and Freddy took them for a cruise on the lake. Of course the outboard motor was pretty small, and the houseboat was big and clumsy, so they went pretty slow—probably not more than a mile an hour. But they all enjoyed it—all, that is, except Uncle Wesley, who got sea-sick and had to lie down on Freddy's bed with a cold compress on his head.

After they had all gone, Freddy felt pretty lonesome. It was all very well to live a nice quiet life in pleasant surroundings with lots of time on your hands to do anything you wanted to do. That was the kind of life he had wanted, and now he had it. But just the same it was pretty pleasant to be with your friends, and to hear all the old familiar jokes. And he began to think rather longingly of the shabby old armchair in the pigpen, and of how he might even now be sitting there and looking out through a rather dirty window, and seeing his friends going about their affairs, and maybe Mrs. Bean coming to the kitchen door and shaking the crumbs off the tablecloth.

His eyes prickled a little, and then he shook his head angrily. "This is the kind of summer I wanted," he said, "and I'm going to enjoy it if it kills me!" Then he laughed. "I do enjoy it of course," he said. "Only it makes me realize how fond I am of my friends when I see them after being away for a while."

He stood for some time at the gate, looking towards the top of the hill over which the animals had disappeared, and he was turning to go back to the houseboat when he heard a car coming. There was something familiar about the sound of that car. It rattled and banged and backfired, and—suddenly it came around the turn of the road and Freddy recognized it. He hadn't seen it in several years, but he recognized it. And ducked back into the bushes.

On the road to Florida, some years earlier, the animals had had a good deal of trouble with a man with a black moustache and a dirty-faced boy. Some of the animals—the more edible ones —had been captured and barely escaped being eaten by these two, and they had been pursued by this same ramshackle car which now came jouncing along towards Freddy. It was such an old car, and had such bad springs that, even though the road was pretty smooth, it bounced and bucked and sometimes seemed to be galloping rather than running on four wheels; and the man with the black moustache, who was driving, and the dirty-faced boy, who was hanging on for dear life, were half the time sitting on nothing but air, a foot above the broken seat.

Freddy had been the fraction of a second too late in hiding himself. The dirty-faced boy had seen him, and as the car jerked past the gate, he yelled: "Hey, pa! There's a pig!"

The man stepped on the brake and stopped the car so abruptly that it slid ten feet, and the dirty-faced boy's nose was flattened against the windshield.

"Where?" said the man.

The dirty-faced boy held his injured nose with one hand and pointed with the other, and then they both piled out of the car. And Freddy jumped out of the bushes and raced down the gravel drive for the safety of the big house.

Chapter 5

As he tore down the gravel drive it seemed to Freddy that the unpleasantest sound in the world was the thump of loud pursuing feet coming closer and closer when you can't possibly run any faster yourself. And this was twice as unpleasant, because there were two pairs of feet. It was a long way from the gates to the house, and the feet were gaining with every stride. Any second Freddy expected that a large pair of hands would pounce upon him, and then a second pair of hands, smaller but dirtier, would grab his legs, and he would be carried off struggling to a dreadful fate.

He could see the kitchen door now. It was open, too. But he would never have made it if the man with the black moustache hadn't suddenly slackened in his stride and put his hands to his throat and begun to cough. For he had been running with his mouth open—which is no way to run, but he didn't know any better—and a pebble that Freddy had kicked up had gone straight down his throat.

"What's the matter, pa?" said the boy, and he slackened too.

But the man waved him on. "Stone—throat," he gasped. "Catch pig."

The boy dashed forward again, and in a second the man followed, but Freddy had reached the door. He tore up the steps and into the kitchen, where Mrs. Winch was frying doughnuts in a big kettle of grease.

"They're after me!" he panted. "Stop 'em." And he pushed through the door that led into the front part of the house, just as the dirty-faced boy reached the kitchen.

"Which way'd he go?" demanded the boy. "Wild pig. We're chasing him."

"I ain't seen any pig," said Mrs. Winch calmly. She turned from the stove to face him, and then she started back and her mouth fell open as she stared in dismay at the man with the black moustache who was standing in the doorway.

The man stared back at her. And his mouth, which he had closed carefully after getting the pebble out of his throat, also fell open. As for the dirty-faced boy, when he saw these two staring at each other without saying anything, his mouth of course fell open too.

The man was the first to recover himself. "Well, well," he said with a sort of ferocious joviality, "if it isn't my own dear lovin' wife, Sarah Winch! What a happy reunion, to be sure!"

" 'Tisn't happy, and 'tisn't a reunion," snapped Mrs. Winch. "I thought I was shut of you for good and all, Zebedee Winch, when I got away from you at last, ten years ago. Now clear out, both of you, before I take the broom to you."

The man grinned. "My, my!" he said. "What a way to greet a husband that's searched high and low for you all these years! And a son that's missed your lovin' care. Horace," he said, fetching the dirty-faced boy a clip on the ear, "shut your mouth and go kiss your ma."

"Yes, pa," said the boy, and went towards Mrs. Winch. But she pushed him away.

"I'd as soon kiss a pig," she said disgustedly. "In fact, I'd rather."

"Oh yes, speakin' of pigs," said Mr. Winch, "that one that ran through the kitchen just now —well, if he's your pet pig, we're sorry, but Horace and me, we ain't had a mouthful of prime pork in a year, I guess. So—"

"You won't touch *that* pig," said Mrs. Winch. "Mr. Camphor'll have the law on you if you steal him." She turned quickly and looked into the kettle, then lifted the rest of the doughnuts out of the fat with a long fork and ranged them on a sheet of brown paper that she had spread on the shelf over the stove. Then she turned back to them. "Zebedee Winch," she said, "I left you ten years ago because I couldn't stand your lazy thievin' ways any longer. I hoped you'd never find me again. As for you, Horace —if you are Horace, which nobody could tell· under six layers of dirt—I couldn't take you with me then. I hoped that maybe some day . . . But I see your father's brought you up to his own way of doing things. As the twig is bent, so it will grow, and he's bent you pretty crooked, my boy."

Freddy, who had crept back to the other side of the door and was listening, felt so sorry for Mrs. Winch, little as he liked her, that he entirely forgot to make a note of this proverb.

"So there's nothing for either of you here," she went on. "And the sooner you're gone, the sooner I can get on with my work."

"Well now, Sarah," said Mr. Winch, "you surely don't think after not seein' you for so long, we'd turn around and go without hardly a Howdedo? No, no; let's make a pot of coffee and sit down and talk things over. And these doughnuts . . ." He took a handful and tossed one to the boy. "Mmmmmm, I always did like nice fresh doughnuts."

Mrs. Winch looked at him steadily for a minute, then she threw up her arms despairingly and picked up the coffee pot and filled it with water and set it on the stove.

Mr. Winch, who had had his hat on all this time now took it off and threw it on the floor and drew a chair up to the table, and Horace followed suit.

"You've got Horace all wrong, Sarah," Mr. Winch said. "The boy ain't anything to be ashamed of; he's smarter than a whip. He's got the lightest touch in a hencoop of anyone I ever see. Can crawl in and pass me out a couple of fat hens without a squawk out of any of 'em. I tell him he's got a great future ahead of him. Anybody that can rob a henroost as neat as that at his age, he'll be able to clean out a bank by the time he's twenty-one."

Mrs. Winch paid no attention to him. She went on with her work. When the coffee was ready she poured two cups and set them on the table.

"Nice place you got here," said Mr. Winch. He took a noisy drink of coffee, then wiped his moustache with the back of his hand. "But it needs a man around the place. Old Camphor being away and all. Somebody to kind of look after all his nice things. Seems to me I've heard he has quite a valuable collection of coins. Maybe you'd show 'em to me." He grinned. "Got kind of a weakness for coins."

"They're locked up where you'll never get at them," said Mrs. Winch shortly.

"I don't want to get at 'em," Mr. Winch said. "I ain't such a fool as to take anything from a house where my wife works as a cook. Not that you'd give me away—"

"Oh, yes, I would," said Mrs. Winch. "Make no mistake, Zebedee; if you steal anything from here I'll go straight to Mr. Camphor and tell him."

"And send your own husband to jail? Yes, and your own son? Oh, no, Sarah, you wouldn't do that. But set your mind at rest," he said, getting up and bringing a double handful of doughnuts over to the table. "We won't touch a thing. You got a nice job here, and we want you should keep it." He stuffed a doughnut into his mouth. "Yes," he said, with his mouth full, "the more I think of it, the more I think it's a fine setup. When would you like Horace and me to move in, Sarah?"

"Move in!" Her voice didn't sound angry any more; it sounded just plain scared. "Why, you can't! Mr. Camphor—"

"Pooh!" interrupted her husband. "Old Camphor'll be glad to have a man looking after the place. And he certainly wouldn't object to your inviting your lawfully wedded husband to spend a few weeks with you. He wouldn't grudge a few extra meals. Now let's see; for supper tonight we'll have a nice roast chicken, with stuffing, and lots of giblet gravy, and onions, creamed . . ."

For the past few minutes Freddy had been making up his mind to a very courageous course of action. He could see that Mrs. Winch was going to have to give in. If Mr. Winch and Horace wanted to stay, there wasn't much she could do about it. Of course she could telephone for the police, but what could the police do? Mr. Winch hadn't committed any crime by just coming to call on his wife. And even if he had, she wouldn't want to send her own husband and son to jail. Freddy knew that it was his duty, as caretaker, to order them off the place. And so, after figuring out just which way he should run if he were chased, he took a deep breath and opened the kitchen door.

"You're trespassing on private property," he said, in a voice which was loud, but I'm afraid quavered a little. "Kindly leave at once!"

"The pig!" shouted Mr. Winch.

"He talks!" exclaimed Horace. And they half rose from their chairs.

"Leave him alone!" said Mrs. Winch sharply. "He's the caretaker. You'll get more trouble than you can handle if you bother him."

"The caretaker? A pig?" Mr. Winch exclaimed incredulously.

So Mrs. Winch explained who Freddy was.

and how he had applied for the job and been hired.

"Oho!" said Mr. Winch, sinking back into his chair. "So you're one of those talking animals of Bean's? You're *that* pig? Yes, I remember you now. Never forget a face. You was kind of standoffish, as I remember—didn't want to come to dinner." He grinned. "Well, I expect maybe you wouldn't have enjoyed it as much as we would. But we'll try to fix it up for another time, hey?"

"I'm not afraid of you," said Freddy, trying hard to keep his legs from trembling. "And I'm telling you, you've got to leave here right away."

"Oh, now, don't be so harsh," Mr. Winch said. "You wouldn't drive us away when we just got here, and we ain't seen our dear wife and mother in ten years?" He shoved his cup at Mrs. Winch. "More coffee," he demanded. Then he laughed and stretched his legs out comfortably in front of him. "No, pig," he said, "we ain't a-going to leave till we get ready. Now you be a good pig and leave us alone, and we'll agree not to bother you. We'll declare a truce, hey?"

"No," said Freddy. "I can't let you stay."

"Oh, no? How you going to stop us?"

"I am not afraid of you," said Freddy.

Mrs. Winch said: "Come outside a minute, Freddy. I want to speak to you."

Mr. Winch looked at her suspiciously, then he shrugged his shoulders and took another doughnut and Freddy and Mrs. Winch went outside.

"You can't stop them staying, Freddy," said the cook, "and neither can I. Maybe I can think of some way of getting rid of them later on, but for the present we'll just have to put up with them. And after all, they won't steal anything as long as I cook their meals. All they want is an easy life, and as long as they've got it, they won't risk doing anything that would get them into trouble."

"I could write to Mr. Camphor," said Freddy.

"What good would that do?" Mrs. Winch asked. "They'd just tell him the truth—that they're my family, paying me a visit. They'd make you look pretty mean."

"But you could tell Mr. Camphor just how things are," Freddy said. "That you didn't want them here, and that they'll steal things—"

"I know they'll cause me trouble," said Mrs. Winch. "But I'm not going to tell Mr. Camphor that. And," she said, looking hard at

Freddy, "you'd better not tell him either if you know what's good for you."

"Well," Freddy said, "I'll think it over." And he went off down to the houseboat. "Oh dear," he said to himself; "this is my nice quiet summer! First the rats, and then the Winches. And I can't get rid of either of them. What did I ever take this darned old job for anyway?"

Chapter 6

Freddy saw that Mrs. Winch was not going to
be any help to him. If he told Mr. Camphor
the truth about Mr. Winch and Horace, she
would say flatly that it wasn't so, that they had
just come for a visit and Freddy was jealous.
And Mr. Camphor would believe her. After all,
he had known her longer than he had Freddy.

Probably Mrs. Winch acted that way because
she was afraid of losing her job. If Mr. Camphor found out what kind of a man her hus-

band was, he would probably fire her. Then she would have to go back and live with Mr. Winch. And she was afraid of Mr. Winch. Freddy couldn't blame her for that. Mr. Winch was a pretty mean man.

"Just the same," said Freddy to himself, "it's up to me to do *something,* and *something* I will *do!*" Having said which, he sat down on his little porch and tried to think what that something could be. But it was getting along towards suppertime, and all he could think of was how hungry he was getting. Of course his lunch had been both large and late, but that didn't make any difference. "That's one trouble with being a pig," he thought; "no matter how much you eat, you're always hungry again in a little while. Though it's nice, too," he thought, "because you enjoy your meals so much."

Of course all this thinking just made him hungrier, and at last he started up towards the house. He walked quite briskly at first, but the nearer the house he got, the less hungry he felt, and the less hungry he felt the slower he walked. Until, when he came in sight of the kitchen door, his appetite was entirely gone, and he stopped. "I guess," he said thoughtfully, "—I guess I don't want any supper."

So as it seemed rather silly to go up and face the Winches again if he didn't want anything to eat, he turned and started back. But as soon as he did that he began to feel hungry again. "Oh, dear," he said, "I guess the only thing is to get close enough to the house so that I don't want supper, and far enough away so that I'm not scared of Mr. Winch." And after a little experimenting he found the exact spot, just where the path curved around to run straight towards the house. He sat down behind a bush and waited.

After a little while the man with the black moustache and the dirty-faced boy came out of the kitchen door. Mr. Winch was wiping his moustache on his sleeve, and they both had crumbs all over them, so Freddy knew they had had their supper. And when they walked down towards the lake, he went on into the kitchen.

Mrs. Winch was washing up a big stack of dirty dishes. She scolded Freddy for being late, but she gave him his supper. "You'll get it to-night," she said, "but in the future, if you're late you don't get anything. 'Tain't part of my job to keep pigs' suppers hot."

Freddy didn't say anything.

"You needn't be afraid of them two," she

said, jerking her head towards the door. "They won't bother you if you don't bother them. Best thing to do is say nothing, just like I'm going to do. What Mr. Camphor don't know, won't hurt him."

Freddy still didn't reply. He ate quickly, went out, and took a roundabout course down towards the houseboat. He was hurrying through a clump of tall elms when there was a sound above him like a hammer striking a piece of wood, and a stone fell at his feet. He looked up. Nailed to one of the branches above him was a small birdhouse, from within which came an agitated chirping. And then there was another *tock*! and another stone dropped through the leaves.

Expert detective that he was, Freddy found no difficulty in figuring out what was going on. Somewhere at a little distance away the dirty-faced boy was throwing stones at the birdhouse.

"Hey! You, up there!" he said. "Come down here. You'll get hurt if you stay there."

A bluebird's head appeared at the doorway, ducked back as another stone slashed through the leaves, then the bird popped out and swooped down to a twig a few inches above the pig's head.

"Oh, dear," she said, "what are we going to do? My husband and I just moved in, and I was just starting to give the place a thorough cleaning when that awful boy . . . Oh, dear, oh, dear, whatever shall I do? My husband will be so angry if he comes back and finds I haven't tidied up! Oh, dear—"

"Stop *twittering!*" said Freddy sharply. "Your husband will be still angrier if he comes back and finds you've been hit with a rock. Where is he? Why isn't he helping you?"

"He went up to the garden to find a worm for supper. Nothing seems to agree with him lately, and it makes him so cross. I thought a nice fresh angleworm—"

"Never mind," said Freddy, interrupting her. "You go find him and tell him I said you'd have to find another place to live. Not around here. That boy's going to be here for some time, I'm afraid, and he'll make your lives miserable."

There was a flash of blue through the trees and the bluebird's husband lit beside her. "What's this?" he demanded. "Who says we can't live here?"

Freddy explained. But the bluebird was inclined to make light of the warning. "Boys always throw stones," he said. "They can't hit anything. As for you, sir, I'll thank you not to interfere in my domestic affairs."

"Have it your own way," said Freddy. "But if you're smart, you'll pull out of here quick. And you'd better warn all the other birds who've started nests on this place, too. I know that boy."

"But I do not know you, sir," retorted the bird. "You had better keep your advice for those who need it. I'll have you know—" He stopped, for they heard footsteps and, turning to look, saw Horace coming towards them. "Perhaps you're right," he said hastily. "Come, Elizabeth." And they flew off.

"Oh, it's you, pig," said Horace. He had a handful of stones. "Let's see how fast you can run. I'll give you till I count ten." He grinned and balanced a stone in his hand.

"If you throw stones at me," said Freddy, "you'll get into trouble."

Horace kept on grinning. "One," he said. "Two. Three . . ."

Freddy got mad. Horace wasn't a very good shot, and the stones were small anyway; even if one of them hit him it wouldn't be serious. But he didn't like being bullied. He turned as if to run away, then whirled and charged straight at the boy.

Like all bullies, Horace was a coward. When he saw Freddy coming for him, he gave a yell and tried to run, but he was too late. Freddy drove right between his legs, and he flew up in the air and then landed sitting down on a protruding root. It was a large root, and it probably hurt quite a lot, but not as much as he made out. For instead of getting up he just sat there howling.

But Freddy kept on going. He trotted on to the houseboat, and went into his living room and locked the door. He sat down for a few minutes in an armchair, then he got up and unlocked the door and went out and shoved at the gangplank that led from the bank of the creek to the deck. He shoved it until the end of it just barely rested on the deck. "There," he said; "now if that Horace tries any funny business, he'll get another bump." Then he locked himself in again.

He felt fairly safe now, but he was not very happy. When it began to get dark, he lit the lamp and tried to read a detective story. But he couldn't keep his mind on it, and after he had read a page he would have to go back and

Freddy drove right between his legs. . . .

read it all over again to see what it was about. About half past nine he heard the clatter of Mr. Winch's car approaching along the road. Evidently he had driven off somewhere after supper and was now coming back. The noise stopped, there was the clang of the big gates shutting, then the car went along up towards the house. "If he's locked the gates, no sense my going up there," Freddy thought. So he read a little longer. Then he put out the lamp and went to bed.

When he awoke it was broad daylight. He lay still for a few minutes. There was something wrong, something different, but he couldn't at first tell what it was. Then it came to him: there were no birds. Every other morning he had spent in the houseboat, that was the first thing he had been aware of—the twittering and chirping and singing of dozens of birds. He liked to lie and listen to it. Now and then one would light on the roof and hurry across it in little quick hops. But this morning not a bird could he hear. The bluebirds must have warned them, and they had all moved away.

"Well," he said to himself, "I suppose I'll have to go up to the house and get my breakfast." He yawned, and then he sighed, and then he got up and washed his face and hurried out on deck. Then he stopped. "There's something I've forgotten," he said. "Now, what is it?" He thought. "Something I have to do before going ashore. What on earth . . . Well, I can't wait any longer. Maybe it'll come to me later." And he stepped on the gangplank. And he and the gangplank went down into the creek with a tremendous splash.

He crawled out on the bank and blew the water out of his nose and shook himself. "Golly, that was it—to pull the plank up before stepping on it." He giggled. "It came to me, all right!"

Then he saw Elmo and Waldo sitting on the bank. If they had laughed he wouldn't have felt so foolish. But they just stared at him with their big bulging eyes, as if they were watching a clown at the circus who was trying to be funny and wasn't succeeding very well.

Freddy stared back for a minute. But you can't outstare a toad. "Well," he said finally, "can't you at least say good morning?"

"Excuse us," said Elmo. "We were just wondering what you were trying to do. We came down to see if you'd decided anything about the rats."

"The rats!" said Freddy. "Oh, my goodness, I've got more important things on my mind than rats."

"Yeah?" said Waldo. "Such as what?"

"Such as these Winches," said Freddy. "Tell you about 'em later."

"What are Winches?" said Elmo.

"I'll tell you after breakfast. Maybe you can help me." He started up the bank.

"We thought you were going to help us," said Elmo, but Waldo said: "Aw, let him go. How could he help anybody—pig that can't keep from falling off his own front porch?"

Freddy went on up to the house. Mr. Winch and Horace weren't up yet, Mrs. Winch told him. "Mr. Winch was up pretty late," she said. "He had to drive back home to get some things."

Freddy knew Mr. Winch had got back at half past nine. He thought that wasn't very late. He guessed that Mr. Winch was lazy and never got up early anyway. He thought too that if Mrs. Winch was finding excuses for him, it probably meant that she intended to let him stay, and was trying to make the best of it. Freddy was pretty uneasy, and he finished his breakfast quickly and went out to make the rounds of the estate.

It was just before noon that Freddy was made a prisoner. He had about decided that the only thing to do was to go back to the Bean farm and get his friends to come help him drive the Winches away. He would have preferred to send a messenger, but now that all the birds were gone there was no one to send. He hadn't seen a bird all morning. There were a few squirrels around, but squirrels couldn't be trusted to get a message straight. The only thing to do was go himself.

He was in the living room, packing up one or two things that he wanted to take back to the farm with him, when he heard heavy footsteps on the deck; then the front door was slammed shut and a key squeaked in the lock. He ran to the window. A black-moustached face grinned at him through the screen.

"Hey!" he said. "What are you doing? Let me out of here!"

"Now take it easy, pig," said Mr. Winch. "We got your best interests at heart, me and Horace. We wouldn't want anything to happen to you, like if maybe you was to decide to run away or something, and then you got lost or hit by an automobile. Your Mr. Bean would feel pretty bad if anything like that happened. No, we're going to take better care of you than that." He grinned again. "Safe bind, safe find," he said. "That's what I always say: safe bind, safe find." And he turned and went away.

"My goodness," thought Freddy, "how silly I've been! Why didn't I go when I had the chance! 'Safe bind, safe find,' eh? Well, I hope that proverb isn't true. But I guess it is. He'll find me when he wants me, all right."

Chapter 7

In spite of the fact that Freddy now had the peace and quiet and comfortable surroundings that he had wanted to get when he applied to Mr. Camphor for the job, he was pretty unhappy for the next few days. The houseboat was too strongly built to break out of, and the windows were too small to crawl out of, and with the birds gone, there was no one whom he could send for help. Elmo and Waldo didn't appear,

Freddy and Mr. Camphor

but even if they had they wouldn't have been much use.

At meal times Horace brought him down a tray covered with a napkin and passed it to him through the window. But the napkin was always spotted with dirty fingermarks, and when Freddy lifted it off, the dishes underneath all bore signs of having been sampled. Sometimes, if there had been something specially good, like strawberry shortcake, there would be nothing but a few drops of strawberry juice left in the bottom of the dish. But even if the things looked undisturbed, Freddy didn't have much appetite for them, knowing that Horace had probably pawed them over.

Freddy was so worried and so bored at the same time that he was at last driven to do some work. He made a list of proverbs to be tested out, and he wrote a rather sad little poem about one of them, "Home is where the heart is." It went like this:

> *The wheels are where the cart is;*
> *The jam is where the tart is;*
> *And home is where the heart is,*
> *But mine is far away.*

I miss the dogs and chickens,
And Jinx and Mrs. Wiggins—
I miss them like the dickens,
*   Far more than I can say.*

The wave is where the foam is;
The brush is where the comb is;
My heart is where my home is,
*   And that is with the Beans.*
I am not one who flinches
When cold misfortune pinches,
But I would not like the Winches
*   Even if they were clean.*

After he had written this he felt better, and
he put on his beret and smock and started to fix
up the portrait of Sir Archibald Camphor. He
patched the canvas, but when it came to painting in the face, it occurred to him that he didn't
know what Sir Archibald looked like. Did he
have black eyes and a full beard, or blue eyes
and a long yellow moustache? Or grey eyes and
no whiskers at all? Being in full armor, with his
vizor up, not much of the face would show, but
some of it would have to. Or would it? Why,
Freddy thought—why couldn't he paint him

with his vizor down? He wouldn't have to paint the face, then—just the steel vizor. Freddy didn't suppose any of those old knights had ever been painted that way, but there was no reason why they mightn't have. If Sir Archibald was a very warlike knight, for instance, and wanted to be painted as he looked just going into a battle, he might be painted that way. Freddy decided to try it.

It took him two days. But he had to admit, when the work was finished, that it was a very fine job of painting. Sir Archibald looked as warlike as anything. It was too bad that there was nobody to show it to. Of course there are some artists who say that they don't care whether other people praise their work or not; if they themselves are pleased with it, that is enough. I am glad to say that Freddy wasn't that kind. He liked being praised just as much as you and I do.

He spent a good deal of time at the window, watching to see if any bird or animal came by, whom he could send to the Bean farm for help. One afternoon he saw a tiny speck, high up in the sky. For quite a while it hung motionless, then it circled slowly. A hawk, Freddy thought. And knowing how sharp hawks' eyes are, and

how curious they are about anything on the
ground that they can't understand, he tied a
handkerchief to one of his paint brushes and
waved it out the window. He waved it quite a
long time, and at last the bird seemed to become interested. He came gliding down on a
long slant of air, and then Freddy saw that he
wasn't a hawk at all, but an eagle.

There weren't many eagles in that part of
the state. Freddy knew of two, and as he was
acquainted with them both he at once became
very much excited. He stuck his head out of
the window and waved more frantically than
ever. And as the eagle soared across above him,
just skimming the treetops, he shouted: "Hi,
Breckenridge!" at the top of his lungs. But the
eagle merely gave a harsh scream and waggled
his wings in greeting, and a few seconds later
he was again climbing up the invisible stair-
ways of the air to his former position.

"Oh dear," said Freddy, "he just thought I
was saying hello. But maybe if I keep on waving . . ."

"What's going on here? Who you yelling at?"
demanded a voice, and Mr. Winch appeared on
the bank opposite the houseboat. He had a
shotgun under his arm.

Freddy had a sudden inspiration. "Why I—I was calling you," he said. "I said: 'Hi, Mr. Winch!' I'm glad you heard me."

"Yeah?" said Mr. Winch.

"Yes," said Freddy. "I wanted to tell you about the lawn. It hasn't been mowed since you got here, and the grass is getting pretty high. If it goes much longer, you won't be able to mow it at all."

"Who—me?" demanded Mr. Winch. "You don't think I'm going to cut all that stuff do you?"

"I'd just as soon cut it," said Freddy. "If you'll let me out long enough."

Mr. Winch thought about it for a minute.

"People going by and seeing the grass so long will think it's queer," Freddy said. "They know Mr. Camphor wants it cut."

"O. K." said Mr. Winch. He let Freddy out and accompanied him to the shed where the mower was kept. "No funny business now," he said as Freddy started the engine and got into the seat. "I'll be watching." And he tapped the gun meaningly.

So Freddy started. He went straight, back and forth, back and forth, three or four times. Above him, the eagle was again a speck in the blue sky. And pretty soon Mr. Winch got tired of standing guard over him and went and sat down under a tree. And Freddy steered out into the middle of the big lawn and mowed the word "Help!" in letters forty feet long.

But something aroused Mr. Winch's suspicions. Perhaps it was the sound the mower made in cutting the short curves of the letters. Whatever it was, he got up suddenly and lounged across to where Freddy was just finishing the p. At first he just laughed. "Writin' a letter to the moon?" he asked. Then he looked up and saw the eagle, who was spiralling downward. "Oho!" he said. He put the gun to his shoulder. "Get down!" he commanded. "Quick! Into the house!" And he drove Freddy before him at a run.

The eagle, with the great presence of mind which all eagles possess, evidently grasped the situation. He folded his wings and shot down like an arrow, apparently attempting a rescue. But before he could attack they had reached the house. As Freddy was prodded through the doorway, he could hear the whistle of air through the stiff feathers as the eagle spread his great wings to brake his fall and keep from driving straight into the side of the house. Mr.

Winch turned, and at sight of the steel-sharp talons spread to tear at him, pulled up the gun and fired. But the eagle ducked at the flash and the shot hissed harmlessly past him. Then with a scream he soared up and over the house.

Freddy spent the next few days locked in a small bedroom on the second floor where at night he could hear Simon and his family scrabbling around in the attic. Except when he was sleeping, and eating the meals that Horace brought him, he spent his time at the window, which looked out over the lake. But though he watched the sky until his neck ached, no floating speck appeared anywhere in the blue. But perhaps Breckenridge had gone down to the farm to report what he had seen. Perhaps even now a rescue party was on its way through the Big Woods. It was this hope that sustained him during the long hours of imprisonment.

On the second morning he heard what he at first thought was a plane, then realized that it was the outboard motor when he saw the houseboat moving slowly out into the lake. Mr. Winch and Horace were aboard; they anchored offshore in front of the house and started fishing. At noon they came back·for dinner, and afterwards they went out again. They caught a

"Quick! Into the house!"

few perch, and cleaned them on the nice white table under the awning where in fine weather Freddy used to eat his supper. It made him pretty unhappy to see what a mess they were making of the boat.

The next morning when Horace brought up the breakfast, he said: "There was a cat came to see you last night. Pa said it wouldn't do no harm to tell you." He giggled. "Can you beat it? A cat coming to call on a pig!"

"Oh," said Freddy breathlessly, "was it Jinx? Where is he?"

"Dunno," said Horace. "He went."

"Went!" Freddy exclaimed. "Didn't you tell him I was here?"

Horace laughed derisively. "You must think we're dumb or something! Nah, pa told him you'd gone. Said you and him didn't get along so good, and you'd taken a job as caretaker on some big place on the other side of the lake. Said a man had come and called for you in a big car. The cat wanted to know where, and pa said it was about eight miles beyond Otesaraga village, and then the cat wanted to know the man's name, and pa said he thought it was Smith." He laughed again. "Pa's smart, all right."

Freddy didn't say anything. If Jinx had been warned by the eagle, he wouldn't be taken in by any such story as that. On the other hand, if he had just come up alone to call, he might believe it. It didn't look too good.

"Say," said Horace, "that's quite a fancy picture you got on the boat. Did you paint it?"

"Part of it," said Freddy. "Why?"

"Oh, I dunno. I kind of liked it. Gee, I wish I could paint like that."

"Well," said Freddy, who thought this might be a way of getting on the right side of the boy, "I guess I could teach you. I mean, I could start you. I'm not really a very good painter—my talents lie elsewhere. But if you want to bring my paints and things up here, I could show you a little."

"Aw, well." Horace seemed in doubt. "I dunno. Pa says painting's sissy. I guess 'tis . . . maybe. Anyway, he says I can live on the boat, and I'll be pretty busy there now." He hesitated a moment, then turned and left the room.

"If I could get that boy away from his father," Freddy thought, "I could get somewhere with him. I have a feeling about him, that he isn't as bad as he seems. He stays dirty and throws stones because his father tells him that's the manly thing to do. Yes, I certainly have a feeling about him."

When Freddy said this he meant that he believed there was a lot of good in Horace if it could only be brought out. And he was probably right. For pigs understand boys pretty well, perhaps because they are so much alike. If fathers and mothers who have trouble with bad boys would consult pigs oftener, they would profit by it. But perhaps that is too much to ask.

Freddy however had no chance to do anything with Horace. That afternoon he heard a car come up the drive. He knew it wasn't Mr. Winch's car, because there was no rattling and banging, only the swish of big tires on gravel. The front door was on the other side of the house, so he couldn't see who got out of it, but he heard doors opening and shutting downstairs, and the sound of quick footsteps, and after a few minutes Horace came out and ran down towards the houseboat. After that there was silence for a long time.

And then heavy footsteps came up the stairs. The door was unlocked and Mr. Winch came in. He looked cleaner than usual—or perhaps it would be nearer the truth to say that he looked less dirty. There were no crumbs on his vest and an attempt had evidently been made to brush his hair and wash his face. But the brushing had only been done in front, so that the back of his head still gave a good imitation of a haystack in a high wind, and his face was just streaky, like a window that has been carelessly washed.

"Mr. Camphor's come back from Washington for a day," he said. "He wants to see you." Then he scowled threateningly. "And you be pretty careful what you tell him, if you don't want to get into trouble. Come along."

Chapter 8

Mr. Camphor sat behind a big desk in his library. Beside him stood Bannister, with his chin up and his elbows out. Evidently Mr. Camphor needed a lot of dignity for the coming interview. On a chair in front of the desk sat Mrs. Winch.

When Freddy came in, followed by Mr. Winch, Mr. Camphor looked up. His expression was so disapproving that Freddy's heart would have gone into his boots if he had had any on, and his tail came completely uncurled, as it always did when he was scared.

"Well, young pig," said Mr. Camphor severely, "what have you got to say for yourself, eh?"

"I—I don't know why you ask me a question like that," Freddy said. "I should think you'd be asking these people what they're doing here, and why they locked me up. I've only tried to do my duty."

"I've already asked them," said Mr. Camphor. "They have told me about your behavior, and I must say I am very much disappointed in you. But I won't dismiss anybody without giving him a hearing. So if you have anything to say, let's hear it."

"I can only tell you just what happened," Freddy replied. And he did, leaving out only the part that had to do with the rats and the secret passage.

When he had finished, Mr. Winch, who had been sneering openly through the recital, said: "Not a word of truth in it, sir. As I told you, Horace and self only came to pay a short call. But when we found the state things were in, and when we realized that Mrs. Winch would be blamed for it, and even perhaps accused of stealing the things that were missing—"

"Missing!" Freddy interrupted. "What things are missing? If there's anything been stolen—"

"Kindly let him finish," cut in Mr. Camphor sharply, and Freddy subsided.

"As I was saying, sir," Mr. Winch continued, "when we realized this, we decided that we had better stay for a while and try to put affairs in order. It wasn't very convenient, right at this time, for I have my own business to attend to at home, but we felt that no sacrifice was too great to make when your interests, as well as Mrs. Winch's, were at stake."

"What can't be cured must be endured," said Bannister.

"Eh?" said Mr. Camphor. "You refer to this pig, Bannister? I don't agree with you. If we can't cure him of his bad habits, we don't have to endure him. We can just get rid of him. Just make a note of that."

So Bannister took a notebook and a pencil from his pocket and jotted it down. Even as frightened and unhappy as he was, Freddy noticed that the man did it without in the least relaxing his dignity, or even lowering his chin so that he could see what he was writing.

Mr. Camphor turned again to Freddy. "You

are not aware, I suppose," he said rather sarcastically, "that some of the most valuable coins
in my collection are missing? Also several suits
of clothes, and a small Dresden china basket
decorated with forget-me-nots and filled with
peanuts, which stood on my desk. Also from my
desk, a purse containing fifteen dollars."

"Who steals my purse steals trash," said Bannister.

Mr. Camphor frowned. "You do seem to pick
very poor proverbs today, Bannister," he said.
"A purse with fifteen dollars in it is certainly
not trash."

"I was referring to the purse itself, sir," Bannister replied. "Not the money."

"Oh," said Mr. Camphor. "Dear me," he
said; "it was a pigskin purse, if I remember cor-
rectly." He looked thoughtfully at Freddy.

"I know the rest of that proverb," said the
pig. " 'But he that filches from me my good
name, robs me of that which not enriches him,
and makes me poor indeed.' And that, Mr.
Camphor, is just what these people are trying
to do. They're just lying about me. I haven't
stolen anything. I—"

"Oh, yeah?" broke in Mr. Winch. "Well, who
else stole the things, then? I suppose you won't

deny that you've been all over the house, sneaking in and out at odd hours? Mrs. Winch has heard you, night after night—"

"Why, Mrs. Winch!" Freddy exclaimed. "You wouldn't have said that! Please, Mrs. Winch—I know you didn't like having me here, but please tell Mr. Camphor the truth. Tell him what you said to me about Mr. Winch and Horace the day they came. Remember? You said you knew they'd cause you trouble, and you'd try to get rid of them. You said—"

"Yes, you tell him, Sarah!" interrupted Mr. Winch. He looked very hard at Mrs. Winch, and after a moment she said in a dull voice: "I didn't say any such thing."

"You was glad to see your dear husband, wasn't you, Sarah?"

"Yes," said Mrs. Winch.

"And you'd heard this pig sneakin' round at night and thought he was stealing things, didn't you? But you was afraid of him, so you asked us to stay and protect you and look after the place. Eh?"

"Yes."

Freddy saw that there was no help to be expected from Mrs. Winch. She was too afraid of her husband, or of losing her job, or perhaps both. Before he could think of anything else to say, Mr. Winch said: "I tell you, Mr. Camphor; if you want to see what kind of a caretaker this Freddy really is, come down to the houseboat. I want to show you how he looks after your nice things."

So they walked down to the houseboat. Freddy was horrified to see the state everything was in. The deck was all tracked up with mud, the white table and gay canvas chairs were covered with fish scales, a few fish heads still lay about in corners, and the white paint about the door was grimy with dirty fingerprints. As Mr. Camphor looked about with a frowning face, Horace came out of the living room.

"This is Horace, Mr. Camphor," said Mr. Winch. "My boy. A good hard worker, Horace is. A chip off the old block, sir."

"He's a rather dirty chip," said Mr. Camphor.

"The dirt of honest toil—nobody can object to that," Mr. Winch protested. "He's been trying to clean up after this pig."

"You can't clean a pigsty without getting your hands dirty," said Bannister.

"Eh? Is that a proverb, Bannister?" Mr. Camphor asked.

"Well no, sir. Not exactly. That is, I just made it up."

"Well, don't make up any more. We have plenty of old ones to examine into without making up new ones. And it's not a very good one anyway."

"Yes, sir," said Bannister. But Freddy noticed that he wrote it down just the same.

Mr. Camphor went into the living room, and the others followed him. There was a good deal of mud in here too, on the chairs even, and everything was in disorder. Some of the books had been pulled out and leaves that had been torn out of them were scattered about. Mr. Camphor gave an angry exclamation as Mr. Winch pulled open the bedroom door and pointed to the unmade bed, from which a mud-spotted down quilt trailed on the floor.

Freddy started to protest again. He had never left the bed like that, he said. But since he had been locked up in the house, Horace had been sleeping here, and—

"Lies, all lies!" Mr. Winch interrupted. "Ain't it a cryin' shame—him so young, and the truth just ain't in him."

But Mr. Camphor's eyes had fallen on the

portrait of the man in armor. "How did that get down here?" he asked.

"I carried it down," said Freddy. "The rats had gnawed a hole in it."

"There ain't any rats in the house," said Mrs. Winch.

"Put his foot through it, carryin' it down, more likely," said Mr. Winch.

"And I thought you said you hadn't been around anywhere in the house?" said Mr. Camphor.

Freddy didn't want to say anything in front of the Winches about the secret passage. "I went up in the attic on account of the rats," he said. "I thought I'd repair this as well as I could but of course with his face gnawed away, I didn't know what he looked like, so I painted it with the vizor down."

"I can see you painted it," said Mr. Camphor, "and a very good job too. But I'm not very well satisfied with your explanation. Mrs. Winch has been in my employ a number of years. I have no reason to doubt her word that there are no rats."

"But there *are* rats," Freddy insisted. "If you'd just go up in the attic, sir—"

Horace and his father had been exchanging

meaning looks, and now Mr. Winch went hurriedly into the bedroom, then called to Mr. Camphor. "Come in here, sir. Here's something you ought to see."

They all went in. Mr. Winch pointed to a drawer which he had opened in the bureau. "I guess this proves what kind of a caretaker the pig is. Lucky I thought to look around a little."

There were some clean sheets and pillowcases in the drawer, and on top of them lay several coins.

"My 1776 dollar!" exclaimed Mr. Camphor. "And good gracious, my gold rising sun doubloon! Well, that seems to—ha, to prove it. What have you to say now, pig?"

"And look here," said Mr. Winch. "Is that the dish from your desk?" And he pointed to a small blue dish full of peanuts which stood on top of the bookcase. Freddy was almost certain that it had not been there when they came in, but there was not much good saying so now.

"Well, pig?" said Mr. Camphor.

"Oh, I don't know what to say!" said Freddy desperately. "Whatever I tell you, these people will say I'm lying. They've just ganged up on me. I don't know how those things got here. I didn't take them."

Mr. Camphor shook his head. "Seeing is believing," he said. "Make a note of that, Bannister. I guess you took them all right, and all the other things that are missing. I realize that I made a mistake in picking you as the one to take care of this estate."

"Care killed the cat," put in Bannister.

"Oh, shut up, Bannister," said Mr. Camphor irritably. "That hasn't anything to do with it. A little more dignity, please, and a little less irrelevance.

"I could, of course," Mr. Camphor went on, "turn you over to the police. But I am not going to do that. And I will tell you why. The loss of the few things that I have missed doesn't mean much to me. I am a rich man—"

"A good name is better than great riches," said Bannister.

"Oh, for goodness' sake!" said Mr. Camphor crossly. "I said I was rich. Who said anything about my good name? Anyway, Camphor's a good name, isn't it? Dear me where—ha, where was I? Oh, yes. Well, I'm going to let you go. I'm going simply to discharge you without references. Now go back to your farm, and don't come around here again."

"You mean I'm—I'm free to go?" stammered

Freddy, who felt that a trial and a long term in jail was the least he could expect.

"You hadn't ought to let him go, Mr. Camphor," said Mr. Winch. "Now if I was in your place—"

"Well, you're not," snapped Mr. Camphor. "And if you were, I hope you'd wash your face and scrub those spots off your vest. Or else wear a veil."

Mr. Winch drew himself up and tried to look dignified. "Mr. Camphor, sir, these are my working clothes. This—if I may put it that way —is my working face. If there's dirt on 'em, it's honest dirt, and will be took off when work is over."

"Yes, yes; I daresay." Mr. Camphor looked at him thoughtfully. "But you have suggested that you might take over the job of caretaker here—"

"At great personal sacrifice," put in Mr. Winch, "and only in order to be near my dear wife." And he leered at Mrs. Winch.

"I don't imagine your sacrifice is more than you can bear," said Mr. Camphor. "The pay is good. And I was saying that the work required of you here is not of a specially dirty kind. So

I do not see that there will be any need for your accumulating as many kinds and varieties of dirt as you now seem to have distributed over your—ha, your person. In short, I think that before starting on your duties, a good soapy shower is advisable."

"April showers bring May flowers," said Bannister.

"I doubt, Bannister," Mr. Camphor said, "if even after an entire month of showers Mr. Winch can be expected to produce a very flowerlike appearance.—Why, what is the matter?" For at the word "shower" Mr. Winch had turned pale and sunk into a chair. Horace, who had been listening, slipped quietly outside.

"Nothing, sir. Nothing," said Mr. Winch, recovering himself. "May have had a touch of the sun this morning. I shouldn't worked so hard in the hot sun, but you know how it is, sir: you hate to leave a job unfinished."

Mr. Camphor seemed little impressed by this noble sentiment. "Well," he said, "we will go back to the house. As for you—" He turned to Freddy, "—I shall expect you to be packed up and out of here in an hour." And he led the way outside.

There was nothing else for Freddy to do. He packed up his paints and his few small belongings in a little suitcase he had brought with him, and went out. Elmo and Waldo were sitting on the bank. He looked at them, but they didn't say anything. Freddy didn't say anything either. What was there to say? But it hurt him when, as he passed them, they hopped around and turned their backs to him. He stopped.

"I suppose you heard the whole thing," he said. "And you can think what you want to. But I'll be back again. I'm not through with the Winches yet. Or Simon and his gang either."

But the toads neither turned around nor replied.

Freddy climbed the bank, but as he started up the drive, Bannister, with a finger to his lips, slipped out from behind a bush. "Excuse me," he said, "but that quotation—about the purse being trash, you know. I didn't get that all down, and I wonder if you'd be good enough to tell me where I can find it? I'm sorry to ask you when you're in trouble, but—well, there's no time like the present, is there?"

So Freddy told him. And when Bannister had thanked him, he went on out of the gate.

What was there to say?

Chapter 9

Those had been very brave words with which
Freddy had said goodbye to the toads, but as he
trotted out into the road with the suitcase in his
mouth he realized that he had nothing to back
them up with. He had been fired for stealing,
and he couldn't even prove his innocence, much
less take any measures against either the Winches
or Simon. Like all people who lead very active
lives, Freddy had had his ups and downs, but I

doubt if he had ever before felt quite as down as he did at this minute.

A sharp *Pssssst!* from a bush beside the road startled him, and he looked around to see two yellow eyes in a small black face among the green leaves. Then Jinx bounded out into the road.

"Hi, old pig!" said the cat, slapping him on the back. "Golly, we've been worried! We thought the old sausage grinder had got you at last."

Freddy winced. It is not very tactful to mention sausage or bacon to a pig. But he was fond of Jinx, and so glad to see him that he couldn't be offended. Jinx always talked in a rather rough way, anyway.

Freddy put down his suitcase. "I've had an awful time," he said.

"Hi, Number Seven!" Jinx called, and a rabbit bounded out into the road. "Back to the farm and tell 'em Freddy's safe." And the rabbit saluted and then leaped the ditch, and Freddy watched him speeding away southward across the fields like a stone skipped over still water. "Number Eighteen!" called Jinx, and another rabbit appeared. "Stand by for orders." Then he turned to Freddy. "What do we do—move in on these birds right away? We can have every-body up here in an hour."

"No," said Freddy. "It isn't as simple as that. How long have you been here, Jinx?"

"Since yesterday. Breckenridge told us you were in some sort of trouble, so I came up with some of the others. I called at the door first—"

"Yes," said Freddy. "I heard about that."

"That dirty-faced boy—I recognized him, but I didn't let on, and of course he didn't remember me—he gave me some song and dance about you moving away. We knew it was the bunk. So most of 'em went back, and I stayed on guard with some rabbits for messengers. Breckenridge's aunt—the one that lives up near Saranac—is sick again, so he had to go up there. That's why you didn't see him again. But suppose you give me the low-down."

"I will," said Freddy. "But I want to get back to the farm. I'll tell you as we go along."

"You can't talk and carry that case," said the cat. "See that clump of trees? Bill's over there, and Peter's behind the wall across the field. We thought if either the boy or the man came out we could jump out and muss 'em up. We didn't want to go inside till we found out where you were. But we'd planned a little commando raid for tonight." He raised his voice and gave a long "Miaouw!" and a goat dashed out from the trees, and a bear came lumbering from behind the stone wall towards them.

When these two had greeted Freddy and told him how glad they were that he had escaped, Peter, the bear, picked up the suitcase and they all started off homeward. On the way, Freddy told his story. "You see," he said, "it won't do much good to raid the place and drive the Winches away. I've got to prove to Mr. Camphor that they lied about me, and I've got to get back the stuff they stole, too."

"They probably sold it," said Bill.

"They may have sold some of it," said Freddy, "but my guess is that Mr. Winch stole mostly things he could take back home and use, like those suits of clothes. He isn't really a professional burglar."

"Just a sort of hobby with him, eh?" Bill remarked.

"You might put it that way. And another thing: I heard their car driving off and coming back about once every day they were there, so I think they stole a lot more things than Mr. Camphor missed. After all, he didn't have time to look around much. And that house is just crammed with things. You could take ten truckloads out and it still wouldn't look as if anything much was missing."

"Well, we know where Winch lives," said Jinx. "We had enough trouble there when we went to Florida."

"Sure," said Peter. "We'll hitch up Hank to the old phaeton and go down there and get the stuff."

"Something like that," said Freddy. "We'll have to work out some plan together. But right now—well, I'm so glad to be getting home that I'd rather not think about those people for a while."

So the rest of the way they told him all the farm gossip.

When they had gone over the hill through the Big Woods, and were coming down through Mr. Bean's woods, Freddy said he'd like to avoid the duck pond on his way back to the pigpen. "Uncle Wesley will want to hear all about it," he said, "and he'll have a lot to say, and I don't want to talk about it right now." So they didn't follow the brook down, but came out of the woods higher up, where Mr. Bean had planted his big Victory Garden.

Some of the vegetables were already coming up, and Freddy stopped to look at the neat rows of green shoots. "My goodness," he said, "Mr. Bean certainly does plant straight rows! And how nice they look!"

"Yeah," said Bill, "and they're going to look a lot nicer if Mr. Webb gets his ideas across." Mr. Webb was a spider who lived in the cowbarn in the summer. He was small and plump and black and he had eight legs, and his wife, Mrs. Webb, looked just like him, except that she wore bangs. They were very popular.

"What do you mean?" Freddy asked.

"Come over here," said Jinx, and he led the pig around to where, on one side of the garden, two tall dead stalks of last year's goldenrod were still standing. Between them he could see that something was hung, something that shivered and shimmered in the light breeze. And then he saw that it was a sign, woven of spider web, like the signs that are sometimes hung out above the streets at election time, telling you who to vote for.

Freddy went closer and read it. "Patriotic Mass Meeting. Tonight at 8:30. All Bugs, Beetles and Caterpillars Invited. Fireworks, Music, Dancing. Mr. Webb will speak."

"I don't get it," said Freddy. "What's he going to talk about?"

"I think he'd like to tell you about that himself," said Jinx. "He's been hoping you'd get back, so you could help him. For one thing, he wants you to type out some signs like this for other meetings. It took him and Mrs. Webb two days to weave this one, and then a horsefly got into it and they had to spend another day repairing it. He wants you to fix up a megaphone, too. If they have a big meeting, those in the back rows won't hear much.

"Look, Freddy. He's asked the animals to stay away, because he's afraid that if we came we might step on some of the audience and squash 'em. But if you make him a megaphone and bring it up tonight, he'll be willing to let you stay and you can hear what it is all about."

Freddy agreed, and they went on down to the pigpen, where he thanked them for their help, and said he guessed he'd go in and rest a while, as he was pretty tired.

"O K," said Jinx. "But don't forget the megaphone. Mustn't let the old boy down."

So a little after eight that evening, Freddy started out. He had the megaphone with him. He had made one the summer before for Jerry, an ant who had lived with him for a while. It was just a cone of stiff paper. If Mr. Webb got down in the narrow end, even with his little voice everything he said would come out good and loud.

When he got to where the sign was hung, beside the garden, he found that hundreds of bugs had already assembled. It was beginning to get dark, and he had to walk very carefully not to step on any of them. He didn't see the Webbs anywhere around, but as he tiptoed along, two large beetles stopped in front of him and waved their feelers.

"Evening, Freddy," said the larger one. He had a rather husky voice which could be heard plainly without using the megaphone. "I'm Randolph—I guess you remember how you helped me with my legs, don't you?"

"Of course," replied the pig. "Nice to see you again."

"This is my mother," said Randolph, and the other beetle tried to drop a curtsey, and immediately sat down hard and then fell over on her back.

"Drat it!" she said.

"Never could get mother to use her legs properly," said Randolph as he rolled her right side up again. "Shove that megaphone around for me, will you? I'm master of ceremonies tonight. Webb'll be along any minute now, so I'd better get 'em ready for him."

Freddy pushed the large end of the cone around so that it faced the open space where the audience was to sit, and then Randolph went to the small end and chewed a hole there and spoke through it. "Ladies and gentlemen! Your attention, please!"

The crowd of insects, who had been hopping and crawling around, stopped and turned towards the speaker.

"Ladies and gentlemen," said Randolph, "as you know, our distinguished friend, Mr. Webb, has called this meeting for a purpose. What that purpose is, he will himself explain to you presently. But it is no secret that his message is a patriotic message. Mr. Webb, with the able assistance of his wife, has gone to considerable trouble and expense to provide you with an evening of very superior entertainment, a veritable galaxy of stars, such a display of talent as I venture to say has never before been brought together. But I must ask you to remember that the real purpose of this meeting is a serious purpose, that Mr. Webb's message is of vital importance to

"Never could get mother to use her legs properly."

each and every one of you, as well as to the great nation of which you and I are humble citizens. Enjoy yourselves, therefore, but when you go home, give serious consideration to the words that Mr. Webb has spoken.

"And now," he said, "while we are waiting, we will have a tune from the orchestra."

Four treetoads, and a dozen or so katydids, crickets and other insects which Freddy didn't recognize, came forward. They took places in front of the megaphone and the largest katydid waved his feelers and they started to play, trilling and chirping and rattling for all they were worth.

"Well, this may be all right," said Freddy, "but it doesn't sound like music to me. Modern stuff, I suppose?"

"No," said Randolph, "it's because you don't hear it as we do. It sounds pretty loud down in the audience. Here, put your ear to the small end of this megaphone."

So Freddy did. The sounds came through much louder to him, and he did think that he could distinguish a sort of tune.

"Well, it's queer all right, and they keep good time," he said, "but it isn't anything I'd pick out to listen to. And say, what is this great message of Webb's anyway, Randolph?"

"Stick around," said the beetle; "you'll hear it." He looked around. "Getting pretty dark; I guess we'd better put on the lights." And he shouted: "Lights!"

Immediately several hundred fireflies, who had been stationed on the tops of the tall grasses that surrounded the open space, turned on their lights. Others on the ground in front of the musicians acted as footlights.

"Here come the Webbs now," said Randolph, looking up to where a huge Luna moth was circling above them. "He thought it would be more dramatic to arrive by plane."

The moth dropped down and lit on the low branch of a small tree that stood beside the garden, and the two spiders spun themselves swiftly down on strands of web. Mrs. Webb swung across and landed on Freddy's ear.

"Splendid of you to make this megaphone, Freddy," she said. "I knew I could count on you if you got back. We were going to try to use a morning glory blossom, and I had one all picked out, but I forgot that the miserable things close up at night. I doubt if it would have been big enough anyway. I'll sit with you while father is talking. You'll stay, won't you? He wants to talk to you afterward."

Freddy said he would. The orchestra had stopped and there was much excited applause—which didn't sound much different to Freddy than the music. Then Mr. Webb took his place inside the megaphone, at the narrow end.

"It is a great pleasure to me," he said, "to see so many familiar faces here tonight, and an even greater one to see so many unfamiliar faces. Although the high quality of the entertainment provided would no doubt have brought many of you here, I am sure that the appeal to your patriotism is the real reason for this huge audience.

"Now my friends, I am not much of a speaker. Let's get the serious part of our program over, and we can devote the rest of the evening to pleasure. As you know, our country is now engaged in a great war. We of the insect world cannot fight. We cannot buy bonds. But there is one thing we can do. Let me explain very briefly.

"One of the most important weapons in this war is food. Our farmers are working night and day to produce food to feed not only our own soldiers and the people at home, but to help feed our allies. They have to raise bigger crops than ever before. And there are fewer of them, because so many have gone into the army. In order to increase the crops, the President has asked everyone who can to plant a Victory Garden. This garden on the edge of which we meet tonight, is Mr. Bean's Victory Garden.

"I see here tonight representatives from every walk of insect life. I am glad of that, for you can all help. Some, of course, more than others. I refer to the potato bugs, squash bugs, cabbage worms, cut worms, leaf hoppers, grasshoppers, caterpillars, and others whose main diet is garden vegetables. Now in ordinary times Mr. Bean does not grudge you what little you eat. It's only when there are too many of you and you begin to destroy his whole crop that he tries to drive you away. But this year I don't think that you should destroy any of the crop. Mr. Bean is rationed in what he eats, and if you are patriotic bugs, you won't object to being rationed too. And I believe that you *are* patriotic bugs. And so I am going to ask you to agree not to eat any vegetables at all this year. I'm going to ask you—" He stopped, as a potato bug in the front row jumped up and began waving his forelegs excitedly. "Yes, what is it?"

"It's all very well to ask us to be patriotic," shouted the potato bug, "but what do you want us to do—starve? You're a spider; you don't like vegetables anyway. Besides, us potato bugs don't eat the potatoes; we only eat the leaves and vines."

"When you eat the vines, the potatoes don't grow," said Mr. Webb. "But nobody's asking you to starve. There are plenty of other things you eat that aren't vegetables. There's nightshade vines, for instance. I know you potato bugs like nightshade, for I've seen you eating it. And there's enough up there in the woods to feed a million of you all summer. There are hundreds of seeds and wild plants in the fields and alongside the roads—something for every taste. There's milkweed, now. Most caterpillars like it. Maybe it isn't quite as tasty as garden vegetables, but I'm sure for the duration you'll all be willing to go without some of the things you like for your country's sake. How about it, bugs? Let's have a show of hands. How many are willing to give up something to help win the war?"

Freddy had never thought of bugs as being specially patriotic, and he was surprised when the entire audience suddenly burst into wild and frantic cheering. Of course some of them couldn't cheer, but they waved feelers and forelegs and the caterpillars reared up and swayed back and forth, and even the little flea beetles hopped up and down like tiny rubber balls.

"Thank you, my friends; thank you," shouted Mr. Webb. "I was sure I could count on you. Now I have only one more thing to say. I would like to have some volunteers who would be willing to go out to other farms in the county and organize other groups like this one. I expect to hold a number of meetings myself—indeed, I have already held a good many—but I can't do it all alone, and moreover, an appeal to give up vegetables would come better from someone who is himself making a sacrifice, than from me, who as our friend the potato bug has remarked, do not eat vegetables. I will arrange transportation, of course, and all other details. Some time, therefore, during the dance which immediately follows, please speak to either Mrs. Webb or me about it." He nodded to the orchestra leader, who at once led his musicians into a gay dance tune. And in less than a minute, every bug in the audience who could hop, skip or crawl, had chosen a partner and was dancing like mad.

Chapter 10

Randolph was one of the first dancers on the floor. He led his mother out and they started a sort of slow prance. At every third step his mother got her legs mixed up and fell down, and had to be righted and started off again. But she stuck to it gamely, and as they were rather heavier than most of the other dancers, they soon had a clear space to themselves.

Freddy was very much interested in the different styles of dancing. The caterpillars faced each other with their noses almost touching, then they would take three steps in one direction, then three steps back, then three to one side and three back. Then they would rear up and bow to each other. It was quite majestic.

The crickets danced in a much less dignified way, whirling and kicking up their feet, and occasionally shifting to a position side by side, when they would give a run and then a high leap, which frequently carried them right over the heads of the other dancers into the darkness beyond the floor. Perhaps the most graceful of them all was a pair of grasshoppers, who danced a sort of tango, with many glides and long steps, and quick turns. Although the floor was pretty crowded, it didn't bother them any, for if other bugs got in their way they just stepped over them.

Freddy, who like many rather fat people, was an excellent dancer himself, was thoroughly enjoying himself and was getting a lot of ideas for new steps, when suddenly a loud crowing voice above him called out: "Ladies and gentlemen. Friends and fellow bugs!" and he looked up to see Charles, the rooster, perched on the low branch above him.

The orchestra stopped, and all the bugs

looked up—some of them rather fearfully, for roosters occasionally like to vary their diet of grain with a nice fat bug, and there were many present who had lost friends and even close relatives gobbled up in this heartless way.

"Friends and fellow bugs!" said Charles again.

"Oh, go away, Charles!" said Freddy. "Why do you have to butt in and break up the party? You're nobody's fellow bug! Go on home, like a good fellow."

"Oh, shut up!" said Charles crossly. "You know I always speak at meetings. I just heard about this one, and I hurried right up here." And he puffed out his chest and began:

"Friends and fellow bugs! It is a great pleasure for me to address such a distinguished gathering this evening. Particularly as I am sure there are few among you who have ever before had the privilege of hearing me speak. Correct me if I am wrong—"

"You're wrong, all right," grumbled Freddy. "Privilege indeed! It's torture!"

But Charles paid no attention. "However, let that pass. Our able, if somewhat prosy friend, Mr. Webb, has outlined for you his plan for helping the war effort. It is a good plan, a carefully thought out plan, a plan which has my heartfelt approval. Yet I believe there is more, much more, to be said."

"If there is, you'll say it, all right," said Freddy.

"My friends," Charles continued, "you are the small people of the world, the humble people. You take no part in great events . . ."

Mr. Webb had hurried over to the nearest firefly and was deep in conversation with him.

"What, you wonder," said Charles, "has the war to do with you? What effect can your tiny efforts have on the march of events? You cannot fight, you cannot drive the invader from your shores—"

"There isn't any invader on your shores," said Freddy.

"As our learned friend observes," said Charles, giving the pig a dirty look, "there is, at the moment, no invader. But if there were, what —what—" He paused, and blinked his eyes, for a dozen or so fireflies had come up and were flying in a circle around his head with their lights on. He took a deep breath. "Yet let me say this, my friends," he went on determinedly, "and I say it in all seriousness. On your shoulders rests a great—nay, a well-nigh overwhelming responsi-

bility. And so I counsel you: put your shoulder
to the wheel, put your hand to the plough, put
your ear to the ground, put your—put your—put
your—" He began to repeat like a phonograph
whose needle has got stuck, and as the fireflies
circled faster his eyes, and then his head, went
from side to side, as if he were watching a tennis
match. Each time as they went by his head went
farther around, as if he couldn't help trying to
keep his eyes on them. "Put your—put your—"
he muttered desperately. And then at last his
head went nearly all the way around and with a
squawk he fell right out of the tree.

Charles picked himself up, but he was so dizzy
that he immediately fell down again. Freddy
helped him to his feet. "Darn bugs!" said the
rooster. "That's a fine way to treat me. Me, that's
the best speaker this side of Albany! Me, who's
responsible for what little patriotism there is on
this farm."

"Rubbish!" said Freddy. "You'd have been
responsible for putting 'em all to sleep if you'd
gone on a little longer."

Charles leaned heavily on the pig. "Is that
so?" he said angrily. "That's a fine way to talk to
one of the most useful people on this farm."

"You're useful all right. You crow in the

. . . with a squawk he fell out of the tree.

morning and wake us up, and you make a speech in the evening and put us to sleep. That's fair enough."

Charles shook himself free. "Aw shut up," he said, and staggered off home.

The dance had resumed, and Freddy lay down and watched again. Between the dances, the fireflies gave the fireworks display. They imitated rockets and Roman candles, and a lot of them took their places on a web in the form of an American eagle that the spiders had spun on the tree trunk. The applause for this was almost frenzied.

Freddy saw the Webbs bouncing around together in the middle of the floor, and as he watched, a cricket cut in and whirled Mrs. Webb rapidly away from her husband. Mr. Webb came back to talk to Freddy.

"Nice party, isn't it?" he said. "But I'll tell you, Freddy; things aren't as smooth as they look. You remember that fresh horsefly, Zero? Well, he's back. He's been away to some school or something, I don't know—but anyway, he's learned to spin webs. Just like spider webs, they are. Don't ask me how he does it!

"Well, for a while we didn't mind much, though he gave us a lot of trouble. Mrs. Bean is proud of being a good housekeeper, and so when we're in the house we just spin a small web, out of sight somewhere. But this Zero, he got in and spun webs all over the picture frames and on the dishes on the shelves, and one night he even spun one on Mr. Bean's whiskers when he was asleep. Of course the Beans blamed us for it, and Mrs. Bean swept all the webs down, including ours. I don't think Zero meant any special harm by it; it's just his idea of a joke. But mother gave him a good talking to. And I guess that made him mad, for ever since we moved out in the cow barn for the summer, he's been making a nuisance of himself. He gets in our webs and tears 'em to pieces, and spins his own webs where they'll bother the animals— over their food dishes and on their faces when they're asleep. And of course they think we do it.

"But the worst is, that just since we started this campaign to get the bugs to stop eating vegetables, he's done everything he can to break it up. He tore down our sign, and we had to weave it over again. And he goes around talking, telling everybody we're crazy, and the little they eat won't amount to anything. He's just plain unpatriotic, Freddy."

"Can't you get the wasps after him, as we did before?"

"Jacob went after him one day," said Mr. Webb. "But Zero has got a lot of webs around in out-of-the-way corners, and he'd dodge behind 'em, and Jacob would go zooming into them. After Jacob had untangled himself from about five webs, he gave up in disgust."

The music had stopped again, and Mrs. Webb came and joined her husband. She sat down and fanned herself vigorously with a foreleg. "Good grief!" she panted. "I'm too old to be cutting such didoes! Though I must say it's lots of fun. But why didn't you cut in again, father? That cricket's a fine dancer, but he's the athletic type. My feet weren't on the floor more than half the time."

"It's good for you, mother," said Mr. Webb, "to get shaken up a little. —Hey!" he exclaimed suddenly. "What's all this?"

A big horsefly had buzzed down in among the dancers, who were applauding for an encore. With his strong wings humming like a little airplane propeller, he skated in circles about the floor, knocking over the other insects, who scrambled to get out of his way. "Hi, folks!" he shouted. "I'll show you some dancing that *is* dancing! Whoopee! Out of the way, strut-and-wiggle!" he cried, barging into a grasshopper couple who were swept aside in a tangle of long legs. "Eee-ee-yow! This is Zero's night to buzz!"

"Come on, mother," said Mr. Webb with determination, and the two spiders left Freddy and made for the intruder.

Flies are rather cowardly insects. Zero must have known that the sweep of his wings would knock the spiders aside before they could close in on him, but when he saw them approaching, he flew up and perched on a tall grass stalk that overhung the dance floor.

"Ha, ha!" he shouted. "Frowsy old Webb and his fat wife! You bugs are a dumb lot to let them tell you what you can and can't do. Is this a free country or is it going to be run by a couple of small-time spiders? Telling you to be patriotic! Patriotic your grandmother! Go on eat what you've always eaten. You bet if old Webb liked potatoes he wouldn't be handing out any such talk. The old kill-joy!"

Freddy thought some of the audience were inclined to agree with Zero. He saw them nodding and talking together. The Webbs were climbing the grass stalk to get at Zero, but before they reached him the fly flew over to the sign the spiders had woven with so much work, and started beating it to tatters with his wings.

"I'll make a sign for you," he said, and to Freddy's amazement he began weaving something in the hole he had torn. He worked quickly, and before the Webbs could drop to the earth and start up after him again, he had finished. The letters straggled unevenly, but they were plain. "Vote for Zero, the peple's frend."

"There," said the fly; "if you want somebody to tell you what to do, hold an election. That's the American way. Don't let some old eight-legged frump without any neck kid you into—"

Freddy had lain perfectly still, and big as he was, Zero had not noticed him. Perhaps the fireflies' flickering lights confused him, for horseflies don't usually go out much at night. But now Freddy stood up suddenly, and with a swipe of one fore trotter smashed the sign and its support and Zero down into the grass.

And now if Freddy had had luck, or if he could have seen better what he was doing, Zero's career might have ended right there. For he was entangled in the grass blades, and Freddy slapped down hard several times, aiming at the sound of frantic buzzing as Zero tried to free himself. And then he did free himself. And as he whizzed by Freddy's ear, he gave again his irritating laugh. "I'll be seeing you, pig. But you won't be seeing me." And his laugh died away in the distance.

Chapter 11

Freddy, I regret to say, went off to bed without giving Mr. Webb's troubles another thought. At least he only gave it one thought, and it wasn't a very important one. This was it: he thought: "That Zero is a nuisance, all right, but flies never stick to one thing very long; I don't believe he'll take the trouble to organize any real opposition to Mr. Webb." And when he had thought that, he turned his attention to his own troubles. And I don't know that you can blame him.

The next morning after breakfast he went up to the cow barn to call on Mrs. Wiggins. She had been his partner for a while when he had been in the detective business, and he valued her advice highly. Like all poets, his schemes were apt to be brilliant, but sometimes highly impractical, and her sound common sense could always be trusted to pick out the weak spots in them. If more poets would seek the advice of cows, they would be less criticized for impractical behavior.

On the way across the barnyard he met Mr. Bean. The farmer stopped and looked at him, puffing at the short pipe that always stuck out through his whiskers as if it grew there. "Hear you got fired."

"Yes, sir," said Freddy.

Mr. Bean puffed some more. "Camphor phoned me. Said you stole things."

"No, sir; I didn't steal anything," said Freddy.

"Told him he was crazy," Mr. Bean's pipe gave three puffs and a gurgle. He took it out of his mouth and rapped it on his knee. "Need any help?" he asked gruffly.

"No, sir," said Freddy; "I think I can manage."

Mr. Bean gave a nod and a grunt, slapped Freddy on the back and went on across the barnyard.

That was the nice thing about Mr. Bean, Freddy thought. He let the animals manage their own affairs. He didn't go giving you help unless you asked for it. As a result, you seldom needed it. Because you knew it was there.

Mrs. Wiggins had already had Freddy's story from Jinx, and she and her sisters agreed that something would have to be done about Mr. Winch and Horace. But she didn't agree with Freddy that a general attack should be made by the animals on the Camphor estate. "In the first place," she said, "Mr. Winch has got a gun, and some of us might get hurt. Not that a few birdshot would hurt any of us bigger animals much, but—" she laughed her big booming laugh, "—us cows couldn't afford to have our beauty spoiled."

"You oughtn't to say things like that, Mrs. Wiggins," said Mrs. Wurzburger. "You make Freddy think we are very conceited." Mrs. Wurzburger never could take a joke, even a small one.

Mrs. Wiggins winked at Freddy. Then she said: "In the second place, you don't just want to drive the Winches away. You want to prove to Mr. Camphor that you aren't a thief. Well, it seems to me that the first thing is to find out where the Winches hid the things they stole."

"Oh, they're probably at their house. You remember that house, Mrs. Wiggins, where Charles and Henrietta were almost fricasseed for Sunday dinner. But we don't want to get the things. If we brought them here Mr. Winch would just say that we stole them in the first place. You want to remember that he's an awful good liar."

"But you've got to know where they are," said Mrs. Wiggins. "They're probably at his house, all right, but 'probably' isn't good enough.—For land's sakes, what's the matter with Jinx?" she exclaimed, as a heartbroken "miaouw" came from somewhere near by.

They all went to the door. On the back porch the cat was sitting by an overturned saucer of milk. Instead of lapping the milk up before it all dripped down and soaked into the ground, he just sat and yowled.

"What's the matter with the big gump?"

said Freddy. "I never knew him to make such a fuss about anything before."

Mrs. Wiggins laughed. "I know what it is. Stay here and watch."

If Mrs. Bean had had a heart of stone, those piteous cries would have softened it. But as she had about the softest heart in the county, she was at the door before the third yowl had died away in a long mournful tremolo.

"Gracious Peter!" she exclaimed. "What on earth . . . Oh, you've spilt your milk! Well, there, there." She bent and stroked Jinx's head. "I'll get you some more." She took the saucer in, and returned presently and set it in front of the cat. "There. I put some cream in it this time. Now for pity's sake don't knock it over again." And she went in. Jinx gobbled the milk quickly, and hardly waiting to finish the last few drops in his usually tidy way, bounded over to the cowbarn.

"Did you see that?" he exclaimed excitedly. "Did you see that, all of you? I guess that proves I was right, doesn't it?"

Several more animals appeared from where they had been watching behind the corner of the barn. "It sure does, Jinx," they said. "You were dead right."

"Did you see that?"

"Proves what?" exclaimed Freddy disgustedly. "If you howl, you get fed. What's so wonderful about that?"

"Well, you ought to know, Freddy," said Jinx. "It's a proverb. You know: 'There's no use crying over spilt milk.' Well, there is some use, all right. I cried over it, and I got cream. That makes another one that's wrong."

"We've made a kind of game of it, Freddy," said Mrs. Wiggins, "since we heard about your Mr. Camphor. We think up proverbs and then try them out. Most of them seem to be wrong. Like 'A cat can look at a king.' Can Jinx look at a king? Certainly he can't."

"He could if there was a king around anywheres," said the pig.

"That isn't what the proverb says. It doesn't say: 'A cat *could* look at a king if he had a king to look at.' It just says plainly: he *can*. Well now, can he?"

"Maybe Jinx isn't the cat they meant," said Freddy. "That's a pretty hard one to prove. Hey, I've got one!"

"Let's have it and we'll try it out," said Jinx.

"A cat has nine lives," said Freddy with a grin.

"Oh, yeah?" said Jinx. "And suppose it was wrong: where'd I be?"

"You'd be famous," said Georgie. "You'd be a martyr to science. The cat that sacrificed himself to find out the truth. Come on, Jinx."

"Yah!" said Jinx, because he couldn't think of anything better to say. But after a second he did think of something. "I've got one for you then, Georgie. 'Any stick is good to beat a dog with.' "

"I'll let you try it if you'll try one I just thought of," said the dog.

"Where's a stick?" said Jinx. "O K, let's have it."

" 'There's more than one way to skin a cat,' " said the dog with a snicker.

"I don't know why all these proverbs are so down on cats," Jinx said. "Aren't there any about cows?"

"How about 'Curiosity killed the cat'?" said Mrs. Wiggins. "I've heard Mr. Bean say that to Mrs. Bean when she asked him something he didn't want to answer. Like what he was going to give her for Christmas."

"Pooh!" said Freddy. "If that was so, Jinx would have been dead before he got his eyes open."

"Yeah?" said Jinx. "Well, maybe so. But I'll tell you one thing I'm curious about, and that's what we're going to do about those Winches." He was serious now, and the other animals stopped laughing and nodded agreement. "I guess we all know what happened at Mr. Camphor's," he went on. "And I want to say for myself, and for every animal on this farm, that we're behind you, Freddy, a hundred per cent. Am I right?"

The others agreed eagerly. "You bet!" "You don't have to be told you can count on us, Freddy." "We're just waiting to be told what to do." "When do we start?"

Freddy had known of course that he didn't have to ask for help from any of his friends. But it was heartening to hear them say so.

His ears grew pink. "Well," he stammered, "I—I—"

"Land sakes, don't thank us yet!" said Mrs. Wiggins. "We haven't done anything. Wait till Mr. Camphor apologizes to you and gives you your job back. Then you can give us all a good big hug. Won't that be something, girls?" she said, and the other two cows giggled happily.

"That's right," said Jinx. "We'll make old

Camphor beg your pardon on his knees before we're through."

"Oh, he isn't so bad," said Freddy. "I mean he's all right. You can't really blame him."

"Well, I dunno," said Hank, who had just come up. "Seems like he ought to have known just by looking at you that you're honest. Though I dunno; maybe he ain't so much to blame either."

Freddy laughed. "You think I've got a kind of criminal look, eh, Hank?"

"I don't mean that at all," said the horse, looking embarrassed. "Now, Freddy, you know I don't. I just mean, maybe he ain't very bright."

"Skip it," said Freddy. "I know what you mean, Hank.—Well, why don't we go into the cowbarn and talk it over? Where are Charles and Henrietta? And, Georgie, round up the mice, will you? They might have some ideas. Goodness knows, I need them. I'd been thinking that we could just go up and drive the Winches away, but after talking with Mrs. Wiggins I see that that wouldn't be much good. We've got to be more subtle."

"Land of Goshen!" exclaimed Mrs. Wiggins.

"If I'm going to have to be subtle, Freddy, you've lost the battle right now. That is if I know what you're talking about."

"I don't think I know myself," said the pig. "But come on; let's go inside and talk it over."

Chapter 12

The chief difficulty that the animals had during the talk in the cow barn was to keep Charles from making a speech. Charles was a good orator, but oratory isn't much use when you are planning a campaign. What you want then is ideas, and lots of common sense. Fortunately Henrietta was there, and whenever Charles jumped up and began to spout about "defending the honor of the Bean farm," and "march-

Freddy and Mr. Camphor

ing out with banners flying to meet the enemy," she would give him a good sharp peck on the side of the head, and he would subside. So they were able to plan two things that had to be done before any direct attack on the Winches could be attempted.

The first thing was to find out if Mr. Winch had hidden the stolen things in his house, which was off the main road, about ten miles south of the Bean farm. "Of course the Winches won't be there," said Freddy, "but the house will probably be locked up tight, so whoever goes will have to get down the chimney. Now I'd like a couple of volunteers. Who'll volunteer to look over the Winch house?"

Nobody answered. The four mice—Eek, Quik, Eeny and Cousin Augustus—who were sitting on a rafter, put their heads together and whispered.

Charles ruffled up his feathers and strutted forward. "I am amazed!" he said. "I am astounded! Are these the animals that fought and defeated the terrible Ignormus? Are these those mighty warriors who marched steadily up to the very muzzle of the gun trained on them from the Grimby house? Where is the old Bean fighting spirit? Well, here is one within whose

proud bosom that spirit still blazes. *I* will volunteer. *I* will go to the Winch house. And if
I cannot get down the chimney, I will break
in the door! I will—"

"You will shut your silly beak," said Henrietta, pecking him sharply. "You! You couldn't
break into a pasteboard box! What's the sense
of their volunteering if they can't get through
the chimney?"

"That's right," said Hank. "Looks like a job
for Santa Claus to me."

The mice had stopped whispering. They
stepped forward as one mouse. "We'll go,
Freddy," they said together.

"Good," said Freddy. "I was sure you would.
Jinx tells me that Breckenridge is expected this
afternoon; he said he'd drop in. He'll fly you
down there and bring you back. Two of you,
that is. I'd like the other two to go with Jinx
and me up to Mr. Camphor's." For that was the
second thing that had been decided upon.

So late that afternoon, although the eagle
had not yet put in an appearance, Jinx and
Freddy, with Eeny and Cousin Augustus riding
on his back, set out. They went up through the
woods and over the hill, and then down past the
Schemerhorn farm in the valley. An old black

dog walked stiffly out of the gate towards them as they went by.

"Why, that's Mr. Schemerhorn's Johnny," said Freddy. "I haven't seen him in a pig's age. Hi, Johnny!"

"Afternoon, gentlemen," said the dog, peering short-sightedly at them. "Oh, it's you, Freddy. How's everyone down at Bean's?" He sat down and scratched his ear with a hind foot.

"Fine," said Freddy. "There's a flea on your ear, Johnny."

"Oh, yes. There's several families of them living with me this summer."

"Why don't you chase 'em off?" said Jinx.

"Oh, I don't mind 'em," said Johnny, scratching his other ear. "Fact is, I'm getting pretty old. Can't hunt any more. So they kind of help to pass the time. Give me something to do." He blinked at them. "Don't suppose you've got a small bone with you?" he asked. "You know old Schemerhorn. He don't hardly even feed himself. When he gets through with a bone it's as bare as a china egg."

"We haven't," said Freddy. "I'm sorry. If I'd known we'd see you . . . But about those fleas, Johnny—you mean you're friendly with them?"

"Sure. Even taught 'em tricks." He grinned.

"Look here." He gave a low growl. And immediately Freddy felt a sharp bite on his back and another on his foreleg, while Jinx whirled quickly and bit at the end of his tail.

For a minute Johnny grinned at them, as they jumped and scratched. The mice fell off Freddy's back and scrambled up on the fence rail to be out of the way.

"Hey!" yelled Jinx. "That's a swell way to treat callers. Call 'em off, will you?"

"Atten-*tion!*" said Johnny, and Freddy saw the fleas, like tiny black specks, hopping through the air. They lined up on a stone in front of Johnny, with one, who was a little larger than the others, out in front.

"Say, wait a minute," said Freddy. "Would they do that for me?"

"Sure, sure," said the dog. "That big one, he's the head man. When you growl at anybody, he gives the word and they go for him. Of course, they don't do any fancy drills or anything like that, but—well, look here." He put his head down close to the stone. "Waltz, boys." And the fleas paired off and whirled around in a dance. "O.K. Now hop." And they all began bouncing about the stone like tiny grains of sand.

"H'm," said the pig. "Very interesting." He looked thoughtful for a minute, then glanced up at the sky, which had become overcast. "Going to rain," he said. "We'd better be on our way. Come on, mice. So long, Johnny."

By the time they got to the big iron gates of the Camphor estate, it had grown much darker, and had begun to sprinkle. Freddy sent the mice in to see if the Winches were around, and when they came back and reported nobody in sight he led them in, and they all sneaked down along the creek to the entrance to the secret passage. Freddy snapped on his flashlight and they went along the passage and up the stairs to the first landing.

Light was coming through the peephole above their heads on the right, and Eeny climbed the rough plank wall and looked through. Then he came down and reported that he had seen into a kitchen where an old woman was cooking supper.

"That's Mrs. Winch," Freddy whispered. "She'll be giving Mr. Camphor his supper in the dining room as soon as it's ready, and then Mr. Winch and Horace will come in from wherever they are for theirs. And when they're all

"Waltz, boys." And the fleas paired off ...

eating, we'll see if we can get into Mr. Camphor's bedroom."

They had to wait nearly half an hour before heavy footsteps and a rumble of voices in the kitchen told them that the Winches had come in. The wall was so thick that they couldn't hear anything that was said. Eeny climbed up again, and after a few minutes, came down to report that a tall man had just carried a tray with some covered dishes on it into another room.

"That's Bannister," said Freddy. "He's taking it into the dining room to Mr. Camphor."

"And that man with the black moustache and his boy are sitting at the kitchen table," Eeny said. "Don't they ever wash up before supper? That boy's hands are so black I shouldn't think he could see to eat."

"I don't suppose he's washed in years," said Freddy. "He's still got that extra black smudge under his left eye that he had five years ago when we went to Florida. Well, let's go."

They went on up to the second landing, and Freddy turned the knob of the door which the toads had told him opened into Mr. Camphor's bedroom. It was a heavy door, but it opened very smoothly and silently, and they crept into a large, pleasant room, paneled in dark wood, whose big windows looked out on the lake, over which rain was now sweeping in gusts. Mr. Camphor's slippers were beside the bed, and his suitcase was on a chair, and on the dresser was an open leather case containing hairbrushes, razor, toothbrush and other toilet articles.

Freddy posted Cousin Augustus at the crack under the door into the hall, to warn them if anybody came upstairs. Then he said, "Now, this is the idea. We open all the dresser drawers and pull some of the things out on the floor, and we muss up the things in the suitcase, and generally make the room look as if a burglar had got in and had been hunting for valuables. Then we take one thing that Mr. Camphor is sure to miss, and while the Winches are at supper, we find the room Mr. Winch is staying in—I think it's one of the small ones at the back—and we hide it among his things." He paused doubtfully. "I don't know," he said. "It seemed all right when we talked it over, but maybe . . . Well, how do you fellows feel about it now? It's an awfully mean trick to play on anybody. It isn't very honest—planting stolen property on Mr. Winch."

Jinx, who had gone over to the suitcase and started to toss things out of it, turned around.

"Oh, pooh!" he said. "That's what he did to you, isn't it? You're just giving him a taste of his own medicine. And I hope it chokes him!" he added vindictively.

"Well," said Freddy, "there's a proverb that says 'Turnabout's fair play.' But I wish—"

"Hey, look," said Eeny suddenly. He went up to the pig and stared at him angrily. "This guy is your enemy, isn't he? Well then, you have to fight him with his own weapons. And if you want to know what I think—well, if you're going to go all honorable and tender-hearted about him, I quit! I resign! I won't help anybody who hasn't the spirit to help himself. Why don't you go down and kiss the guy?"

"That's the talk, mouse," said Jinx. "Come on, get busy, Freddy. Hey, what'll we take? Do you think he'll miss these cuff links?"

"He might not," said the pig. "Razor? No, we want him to miss it tonight, and he probably won't shave till morning."

"How about the toothbrush?" said Eeny. "He'll certainly miss that."

"Yes, he'll miss that all right. But nobody could imagine Mr. Winch stealing a toothbrush. It's about the last thing he'd ever take. Why can't we roll up the whole case and take it along?

He's sure to miss something in it. Then we'll hide it in Winch's room and bring something of his back here so it'll look as if he'd dropped it when he was hunting around." As he talked, he pulled out a dresser drawer and tumbled the contents about. "And then we'll sneak back into the passage and listen to the fun." He turned to glance at the door by which they had entered, and then suddenly fell back against the dresser. "Oh, golly!" he exclaimed. "We're sunk!"

At the consternation in his voice, Jinx and Eeny turned quickly towards him, then, following the direction of his horrified stare, towards the door into the secret passage. And they saw at once what had happened. Without their thinking anything about it, the door had swung shut behind them with a faint click, as they entered. And now there was no door. Merely a panel in the wall, like every other panel all around the room. There was no knob or latch or anything.

"I ought to have remembered," said Freddy. "We should have propped it open. Of course. A secret door wouldn't have a knob on the inside. And now how do we get out of the house?"

Chapter 13

Freddy knew that there must be a secret spring
somewhere near the door. If they could find it
and punch it, the door would open and they
could get back into the passage. "I wish we
dared turn on a light," he said, for although it
was only a little past six, the heavy rain clouds
had rolled up so thickly that it was almost as
dark as night. And though they hunted over
every inch of the paneling they couldn't find
any spring.

"This is bad, Freddy," Jinx said. "If you're caught here now, Mr. Camphor will be surer than ever that you are a thief. The mice and I are all right; we're small and dark; we can sneak around and hide and wait for a chance to escape. But you're so large and white."

"If anybody sees you," said Eeny, "you could go. 'Who-o-o!' and pretend you're a ghost."

"Yeah," said Jinx sarcastically, "or he could climb up on the bed and act like a pillow."

Freddy had abandoned the search for the spring and had gone into the closet where Mr. Camphor's suits were hung up. He came out pulling on a pair of dark trousers. "At least I can put on something dark," he said. "Thank goodness Mr. Camphor is a small man. Well, we'll have to give up our plan now, and—"

A warning squeak from Cousin Augustus interrupted him, and the mouse darted towards them. "Someone coming," he whispered, and indeed they could hear footsteps coming up the stairs.

Jinx and the mice dove under the bed and Freddy ducked back into the closet just as the hall door opened and Bannister came in. The man picked up a cigar case that was lying on a table by the window, but as he turned to go he noticed the open dresser drawers. Then he saw the things that had been tossed out of the suitcase. "Dear me!" he said. "Good gracious! Tut, tut, tut!"

He stood for a minute frowning around at the disorder of the room. "Those Winches!" he said under his breath. "Couldn't be anybody else. And I *told* Mr. Camphor—" He stopped with a fearful glance towards the bathroom door. It was plain what he was thinking. Perhaps the thief had not had time to escape. Perhaps he was hiding in there. He took a step forward, then stopped. "H'm, no," he muttered. "Discretion is the better part of valor." And he went hastily out of the room.

Freddy came out of the closet putting on a dark coat. He had found an old cap which was pulled down over his eyes. "Come on," he said. "Let's get out of here. And we'd better split up. It's every animal for himself now. If we get away, we'll meet in the entrance of the secret passage."

Jinx and the mice hurried down the hall towards the stairs, for if they could reach the ground floor they would have a chance of finding an open door or window. But Freddy didn't dare follow them. Besides, he wanted to hear what Mr. Camphor would say when he found that someone had been going through his things. He went back and hid in a linen closet next to Mr. Camphor's room.

Pretty soon, footsteps came upstairs and went in next door. Freddy put his ear to the wall and heard Mr. Camphor say: "Yes, yes, Bannister; I can see for myself that someone has been here. But why do you think it was Mr. Winch or Horace? They're in the kitchen, and Mrs. Winch says they've been there all the time."

"Blood is thicker than water," said Bannister.

"I suppose you mean that she won't tell on her own relatives," said Mr. Camphor.

"Of course she won't. And another thing, sir —she's afraid of them. I've seen the way she looks at them. And my guess is that they had a lot more to do with all the things that were stolen from the house than the pig did. All those suits of yours, sir. What would a pig want with suits? He couldn't wear them."

"Oh, couldn't he!" Freddy thought. "It'll be just too bad if they catch me now, and with one of his suits on. I'd never be able to prove my innocence after that."

"Well, I don't know, Bannister," said Mr. Camphor. "It's true, I liked that pig. He seemed a very sensible animal. And I certainly couldn't ever get very fond of Mr. Winch or that dreadful boy. But there are lots of people I'm not fond of who aren't thieves. What's that?" he exclaimed suddenly.

Freddy had got a crick in his neck from holding his ear to the wall, and in turning to get the other ear into position had knocked over a broom.

"Oh, golly!" he thought. "Now I *am* in for it!"

And he certainly was. A few seconds later the door of the closet was pulled open.

"You!" shouted Bannister. "Come out!" He held a large poker which he shook threateningly at the pig.

Freddy was pretty scared, but he did not lose his head. In his detective work he had often worn disguises of different kinds, and he knew that it was fairly easy to make people think he was a boy or a very small man, if he acted the way they would expect a boy or a man to act under the circumstances. In a coal mine, for instance, you expect to see miners, and if you saw a pig in working clothes, with a pickaxe over his shoulder, the chances are that you wouldn't notice that he was a pig. Because you don't expect to see a pig in a coal mine.

Now Mr. Camphor and Bannister obviously expected to see a burglar come out of the closet, so Freddy decided at once to act as much like a burglar as possible. And there was just the chance that he might manage to fool them. He hunched his shoulders and kept his head down as he slouched out into the hall.

"What are you doing there?" Bannister demanded.

Freddy keyed his voice to a whine, as unlike his regular tones as he could make it. "I ain't done any harm. I ain't stolen anything, Mister."

"Bring him in here," said Mr. Camphor from the bedroom door. "Let's take a look at him."

Bannister motioned Freddy into the bedroom. Fortunately it was now pouring hard outside. The rain drove and rattled against the windows, and it was so dark that whatever look they took at him certainly wouldn't be a very good one.

"Sit down in that chair," said Mr. Camphor, and with a sinking heart Freddy saw him pull the chain of the lamp on the table beside him.

But the light didn't go on. Mr. Camphor tried it twice, then he tried the overhead light, but nothing happened.

"That's a fine thing!" he said. "Lights go off just when we need them. I suppose it's this storm. Well, young man," he said sternly, "what have you got to say for yourself?"

It seemed to Freddy as if Mr. Camphor was always asking him this question. "I ain't got anything to say," he whined. "I just come to visit my uncle."

"I'm not your uncle," said Mr. Camphor.

"No, Mister. Old Winch is my uncle. I come to visit him."

Bannister and Mr. Camphor looked at each other. And Mr. Camphor said, "And did you expect to find him in the linen closet?"

"I thought it was the door to the back stairs," said Freddy. "That's why I went in there."

"That's not very likely," Mr. Camphor said. "And it doesn't explain what you were doing upstairs in the first place. Or what you were looking for in my dresser and my suitcase. Come, come, my man; you can hardly expect us to believe that you're anything but what you appear to be."

"And you certainly appear to be a burglar,"

said Bannister. He turned to Mr. Camphor. " 'Burglars of a feather,' you know, sir."

"It's 'birds of a feather,' Bannister," Mr. Camphor corrected him. "Yes. Quite so. They flock together, you think?"

"Yes, sir. I mean if this burglar is Mr. Winch's nephew, it is quite likely that Mr. Winch is also a burglar. In his spare time, at least."

"That's an interesting thought," said Mr. Camphor. "And in that case, Mr. Winch may very well have sent him up here while we were at supper. H'm. Bannister, you watch this fellow while I go down and call the police."

"Better let me go down, sir," said Bannister. "The stairs are dark, with no lights on. You might slip—"

"Oh, of course if you're afraid to stay with him!" Mr. Camphor said.

"Who—me, sir? Afraid of a burglar? I'd as soon be afraid of a mouse as this fellow! I was merely thinking of your welfare. If you were to fall on the stairs! Old bones are brittle, sir."

"My bones are no older than yours," Mr. Camphor snapped. "Now you do as I tell you." And he went out into the hall.

Bannister pulled a chair into the doorway and

sat down on it. He had a tight grip on the poker, and he watched Freddy narrowly. But presently, a puzzled frown appeared on his face. "Something familiar about you, burglar," he said. "Something—h'm, seen you before. But where? Take that cap off and let's have a look at your face."

"I don't want to take it off," said Freddy. "My—my hair isn't brushed."

"I guess you're no relative of the Winches if you're so particular about your hair," said Bannister. "Maybe you look like your uncle; maybe that's where I think I've seen you before."

Freddy didn't answer. In the shadows behind Bannister's chair he had seen something. It was hardly even a movement—just a slight deepening of the shadows, but he thought he knew what it meant. A mouse, or a black cat, moving in the dimness, would make just such a flicker, so faint that the next moment you were sure that you had seen nothing.

And then he saw the mice. They had crawled up the back of the chair and were sitting on top of it, and on a level with Bannister's ears. They were poised there for a moment, and then they jumped. Eeny landed on Bannister's right shoulder, and Cousin Augustus landed on his left shoulder, and they scampered quickly up his neck and across his ears to the top of his head and jumped off again on to the chair back. And at the same moment, Jinx, just behind the chair, let out an ear-piercing screech.

Most people will yell if a mouse runs across their face; and I guess most people will jump if a cat screeches suddenly behind them. But for a second—and it was a good long second, too—Bannister just didn't move a hair. Then he just sort of exploded. He let out a yell that made Jinx's shriek sound like a three months old kitten crying, and he shot up out of the chair to his full height and about a foot beyond it, for both feet left the floor. But when they came down they were running, and as soon as they hit the floor again Bannister tore once right around the room, and then out the door and down the hall. He was gone almost before the poker hit the carpet.

"Run, Freddy!" called Jinx. But Freddy didn't need any instructions. He dashed down the hall, throwing off the coat and cap, and he fell halfway down the stairs before he got to his feet. But somehow he managed to get the dark trousers off before he reached the bottom. "You never know what you can do till you try," he thought.

From somewhere in the front of the house he could hear Mr. Camphor shouting into a phone, so he turned and made for the kitchen. This wasn't as foolish as it may seem, for he knew that although the Winches were in the kitchen, he could get past them before they could grab him, and the kitchen door opened outward, and had a latch that could be quickly lifted.

And that was the way it happened. The Winches jumped to their feet, but Freddy darted through, with Jinx beside him. And before they knew what had happened, the two animals were safe outside.

"Down to the secret passage," Freddy panted. "They won't find us there. Oh, golly, where are the mice?"

"Don't worry about them," said the cat, loping along easily beside Freddy with his ears held close to his head to keep the rain out of them. "Those lads can take care of themselves. Boy! Did we give old Bannister a lift! He went up like a skyrocket. Lucky we came back to see where you were."

"You certainly saved me just in time," said Freddy. "And it was a good thing the lights went off, too. I suppose it was the storm."

"Storm, nothing!" said the cat. "I turned 'em

He shot up out of the chair . . .

off. We were poking around in the cellar and I saw the switch. I thought it might be just as well to cut the lights off. I don't know much about electricity, but boy, I know more than I did! Because I touched the wrong thing first. Next thing I knew, I was sitting across the cellar with sparks hopping around in my whiskers like those trained fleas of Johnny's. But I went back and got it right the next time."

Freddy saw that Jinx expected to be praised for this courageous action, and indeed he deserved praise. So as soon as they reached the shelter of the passage entrance, he praised him. He praised him up and down and crossways, and pretty soon Jinx got tired of it. "Oh, lay off," he said. "I'm not as wonderful as all that."

Freddy grinned. "All right," he said. "Then let's get along upstairs."

"Upstairs!" Jinx exclaimed. "You mean we're going back up *again*? Didn't you have enough fun last time, so you want to try it over? What do we do—keep this merry-go-round up all night?"

"Oh, shut up," said Freddy good-naturedly. "And come on."

Chapter 14

Freddy had lost his flashlight, so he and Jinx had to feel their way through the passage and up the stairs. Even a cat cannot see anything in complete darkness, although all cats pretend that they can. But they reached the first landing without making any noise. Light was coming through the little hole from the kitchen, so they knew that someone had gone down to the cellar and thrown the switch on again. But they couldn't hear any voices, so they went on up to Mr. Camphor's door.

Freddy cautiously opened it a crack and peered in. There was no one there. But from under the bed came a faint, inquiring squeak, and as Freddy pushed the door a little wider the two mice ran over to him.

"We thought you'd come back for us," they said. "Are you going on with your plan now?"

"We can't take the chance," Freddy said. "Too many people roaming around the house. But I think it's a good idea to stick around and see what happens. Bannister has begun to get suspicious of the Winches, and maybe Mr. Camphor will too."

So they went back into the secret passage and waited. They waited for more than an hour before anything happened. Then they heard footsteps and voices, and several people came into the bedroom.

Very carefully, Freddy opened the door a crack. And the first person he saw was his old friend, the sheriff, from Centerboro. Evidently Mr. Camphor had sent for him.

Mr. Camphor was there too, and Bannister, and the Winches.

"Well, sir," the sheriff was saying, "you say you caught this feller in the linen closet, and then while you was telephonin' me, and while your butler, here—Bannister, is it?—was standing guard over him, he escaped."

"That's it, sheriff," said Mr. Camphor.

"He came right through the kitchen," Mrs. Winch said. "And what's more, we recognized him. He was that pig, Freddy."

"That's right," said Mr. Winch.

"Ah," said the sheriff. "Former caretaker here, wasn't he? And you fired him because he'd been stealin' things. Now that's a funny thing, Mr. Camphor. I've known that pig for a number of years, and I ain't ever known him to do a dishonest thing. When I heard about this yesterday, I said to myself, 'Sheriff,' I said, 'there's something funny about this.' Why, I'd trust that pig with my last cent."

"Just shows you how wrong you can be about people, sheriff," said Mr. Winch.

"I ain't usually very wrong about people," replied the sheriff, and he looked very hard at Mr. Winch, who after a second dropped his eyes and blew out his moustache in an embarrassed way.

"No," the sheriff went on, "I had a lot of experience sizing up people." And he continued to stare, until Mr. Winch, to hide his embarrassment, turned and caught the dirty-faced boy a clip alongside the head. "Don't fidget, **Hor-ace!**" he said crossly.

"Well, sheriff," Mr. Camphor said, "I had somewhat the same feeling about that pig. And I may say I was very much disappointed when I found out that he was not to be trusted. And you tell me he has never been known to steal things before?"

"There always has to be a first time," put in Bannister.

"Maybe," said the sheriff. "But if that's so for Freddy, it's so for everybody here—including Mr. Camphor. I suppose you wouldn't care to say that Mr. Camphor is going to begin takin' things?"

"Dear me, dear me!" Bannister exclaimed, growing flustered. "Certainly not! Mr. Camphor, sir, I hope you don't think—"

"Oh, keep still, Bannister," interrupted Mr. Camphor. "I don't think one way or the other. Maybe you're right, and before long we'll begin stealing little things from each other. I want to find out what the sheriff thinks about this business."

"I think somebody ain't tellin' the truth," said the sheriff. "Here you capture a burglar, and he escapes, and on the way downstairs he turns into a pig and runs out the kitchen door. Now I like fairy tales, Mr. Camphor; after a hard day's work at the jail, there's nothing I like better than just to take my collar off and set back in my chair with my feet on the mantel and read a good fairy tale book about enchanted princesses and such. And if you folks want to tell me a fairy tale about an enchanted burglar, why I'll set down and light my pipe and enjoy it. But if you're going to tell me all this really *happened* the way you tell it, I'll go get in my car and drive back to Centerboro."

"But it was a pig, I tell you," asserted Mr. Winch. "We all three of us saw him. And we recognized him, what's more."

Mrs. Winch and Horace nodded agreement.

"Well," said the sheriff, "there's just one question I want to ask you, then. This pig was in the house. We'll say, for the sake of argument, that he was disguised, because you found the suit and the cap he wore on the stairs. But I've been around and looked at all the doors and windows. They're all locked. All except the kitchen door. And the question is: how did he get into the house in the first place?"

"My goodness," said Mr. Camphor, "I never thought of that. He couldn't have got in except through the kitchen door. And you were in the kitchen all the time, Mrs. Winch, weren't you?"

"He couldn't have got in through the kitchen door," Mrs. Winch said. "I'd have seen him."

The sheriff raised his eyebrows and looked at Mr. Camphor, and Mr. Camphor nodded. "You're right, sheriff," he said. "The only way he could get in was for someone to let him in through the kitchen. That is, Mr. Winch, Mrs. Winch or Horace. Now which one of you was it?"

"I certainly didn't let any pig in," said Mr. Winch sullenly. "Neither did I," said Mrs Winch and Horace together.

"We have only your word for it that he was a pig," said Mr. Camphor. "And, as I told you, he said when we caught him that he was your nephew."

"I haven't got a nephew," said Mr. Winch.

"Pigs and nephews and kitchen doors," said Mr. Camphor. "I'm all mixed up. What do you make of it, sheriff?"

"Well, sir," the sheriff replied, "this is what I make of it. We know there was a burglar, because you saw him. We know he got away, because he ain't here. We know he had to leave by

the kitchen door, and we know the Winches saw
him when he left.

"Now they say he was a pig. But if he was a
pig when he went out, he must have been a pig
when he came in. Ain't that so?"

Mr. Camphor and Bannister nodded agreement.

"All right. But the Winches say no pig came
in, and I think that part of their story is true,
because they certainly wouldn't have let Freddy
or any other pig come into the house. Yet, whoever your burglar was, he had to come in through
the kitchen door, so they must have let him in.
Well, let's see—where was I? I'm getting kind of
mixed up myself."

"I see what you're getting at, sheriff," said
Mr. Camphor. "The only way for the burglar
to get in was for the Winches to let him in. They
wouldn't have let in a pig, or anybody they
didn't know. So they must have let in some burglar that they knew, and then let him out again.
And they lied about his being a pig, in order to
cast more suspicion on Freddy."

The sheriff said: "That's right. I couldn't have
put it clearer myself. And so I think, sir, I'd better take the three of them down to the jail."

"You can't do that," protested Mr. Winch,

who was beginning to perspire. "We ain't done anything."

"Ain't you?" said the sheriff mildly. "Well, then you ain't got anything to be afraid of. But until we get this straightened out, I'm going to take the three of you down and hold you as accessories before, during, and after the fact, as well as on suspicion of contempt, prevarication, tellin' fairy stories, and just common ordinary lyin' to the lawfully elected sheriff of this county. And I shall hold you there pending trial before a suitable court on the charge of burglary in the first, second and third degrees, with complications as hereinbefore stated, on information supplied by Mr. C. Jimson Camphor, hereinafter to be known as the party of the first part, his heirs and assigns forever."

"Golly!" Jinx whispered. "I wish Charles could have heard that!"

The sheriff had found that the language of the law is pretty terrifying to guilty people, and so in cases like this he always used it. But there is one great trouble with the language of the law. The sentences are so long that very few people except judges can get through them without stopping to take a breath in the middle. And of course this spoils their impressiveness. So in his last sentence, the sheriff had not stopped, but had used up all his breath right down to the bottom of his lungs, with the result that he was unable to conclude, as he should, by glaring sternly at the culprits. He merely sank down in a chair, whooping and gulping to get his breathing started again.

But the Winches were scared all right. Mr. Winch fumbled nervously with his moustache, and Horace began to snivel, and Mrs. Winch to tremble. They shot little nervous glances at one another, and then Mrs. Winch stepped forward.

"I've had enough of this," she said. "I've stood between you and the law, Zebedee Winch, and I've covered up your goings on and lied for you to Mr. Camphor, but there's one thing I ain't going to do for you—I ain't going to jail. Now, Mr. Sheriff, and Mr. Camphor, sir, I don't know anything about what happened today. I didn't see anybody go into the house, and I did see a pig go out. But I'm going to tell you the truth about what happened when my husband first came here. That pig never stole anything—"

Mr. Winch, who had been staring at his wife with growing anger and consternation, suddenly grabbed Horace by the arm, and before anybody could stop him, made a dash for the door. He shot through it with the boy trailing behind like the tail of a comet, and was gone.

"Quick, Jinx—the gates! We must close them!" said Freddy. And the two animals started down the stairs, followed by the mice. But they had no flashlight, and though Freddy wouldn't have minded falling down the stairs to save time, they didn't want to be heard, so they had to feel their way. And when they had got out of the passage, and were running up from the creek bank to the gates, they saw Mr. Winch's dilapidated car just going between the gateposts.

The rain had stopped, and through the ragged clouds in the west, the low sun shone out, turning the trees and the bushes and the car and Mr. Winch, and even Horace, to gold. And the car gave a jerk and a sputter, and bounded off down the road.

Freddy sat down on the grass, although it was still wet from the rain. "Oh, dear," he said, "now they'll get away, and I'll never be able to prove to Mr. Camphor that I didn't steal his stuff."

"Oh, don't be so gloomy," said the cat. "After Mrs. Winch tells him the truth— Hey, look!" he exclaimed suddenly, and began waving his paws frantically at the sky.

Freddy looked up, and there was the eagle,

Breckenridge, cruising along just above the tree-tops. When he saw them, he banked sharply and lit on a dead branch just over their heads. "Ah, Frederick," he said in his harsh voice. "And you, my feline friend. I trust that everything proceeds to your satisfaction in the halls of the wealthy Camphor? I have been searching for you."

"Did you take the mice down to the Winches'? Did they find anything?" they asked excitedly.

"All was as you, with your truly remarkable foresight, had predicted," said the eagle, who always spoke in this very flowery fashion. "Your young friends, with a fortitude out of all proportion to their size, descended by way of the chimney. They found much to criticize in the house-keeping, I am given to understand. But after a prolonged search they discovered large quantities of plunder—much of it merely heaped up in the bathtub. Which indicates quite sufficiently, I feel, the character of this Mr. Winch and his offspring."

"Yes," said Freddy, "they don't use the tub much, I guess. But that's swell, Breckenridge. And we must—" He stopped, realizing that the eagle would expect him to reply in the same high-flown manner. "I speak not only for myself," he said, "but for all my friends when I say

that we are eternally grateful for your ungrudg-
ing and exceptionally able assistance in this difficult matter. And your revered aunt, I trust, is
much improved?"

"Thank you," said Breckenridge. "She is indeed completely her old self again. Quite capable, as she says in her quaint way, of tearing a
rabbit with the best of them. But who is this that
approaches at such reckless speed?" he exclaimed. "Ah, the estimable sheriff." And indeed it was the sheriff's car which now came
puffing through the gate.

Freddy went out into the road and waved, and
the sheriff slowed down. "Hop in," he said.
"Thought you must be around somewhere, with
all this talk of pigs." And as they clambered
aboard he stepped on the accelerator. "Got to
catch Winch if I can. Hold on tight."

This instruction was hardly necessary, for the
sheriff's car was even older than Mr. Winch's
and, though not as noisy, much slower.

Breckenridge rose from the branch with a lazy
sweep of his great wings. "I will seek to detain
the fugitive," he shouted, and in no time at all
he was out of sight.

Freddy told the sheriff what the mice had discovered. "But you'll never catch him in this

"Ah, Frederick, and my feline friend."

car," he said. "He's got a good start already, and he can get home and load the stuff into his car and get away before we get there."

"Can't do more'n try," said the sheriff.

They crawled up a long hill at five miles an hour. At the top, the sheriff let out the clutch and they coasted down the other side.

"Look!" said Jinx.

Ahead of them the road ran straight across a wide valley, and halfway across they saw Mr. Winch's car, bounding along at what even at that distance seemed greater speed than they were making, even downhill.

"Oh dear!" said Freddy; and then he said, "Oh gracious!" For a black speck from high up among the torn rags of the storm shot suddenly earthward, aiming for the Winch car. It came down like an arrow, seemed almost to touch the car, which swerved dangerously, then swooped up again.

"He's dive-bombing them!" Jinx exclaimed. "Boy, what a sight!"

Three times the eagle dove, and the third time the car shot right across the road and jounced into the ditch and stopped.

When Freddy and Jinx and the sheriff came up, Mr. Winch and Horace were still sitting in their car. They hadn't tried to escape, and for a very good reason. Breckenridge was perched on the top, just over the windshield.

"O.K., sheriff," said Mr. Winch bitterly. "I'll go quietly, if you'll just drive that trained buzzard of yours off. He darn near scalped me."

The sheriff thanked the eagle, who said, not at all, he was only too happy to oblige the law, and when he had flown off, Mr. Winch and Horace were transferred to the back seat of the sheriff's car and they started on.

Mr. Winch was at first inclined to be belligerent. The sheriff had nothing on him, he said. "And I guess you see now," he said, "that we were telling the truth about this pig. He was in the house all right."

Freddy started to say something, but the sheriff nudged him and said, "Where he was or where he wasn't has nothing to do with the case. Nothing was stolen today, so even if he had been in the house, which he doesn't admit, there's no charge against him."

Mr. Winch continued to bluster, but when the sheriff, instead of going on towards Centerboro and the jail, drove up the road where he lived and where the stolen goods were parked, he got pretty nervous. And when finally, inside the house, he was confronted with all the things he had taken from Mr. Camphor, he broke down and confessed. And the sheriff drove him and Horace to the jail and locked him up, and then drove the animals back to the farm.

Chapter 15

In the pale dawn light of the next morning, Charles, the rooster, hopped down from the fence, after he had crowed three times to wake everybody up and get the work of the farm started, and walked over towards the pigpen. Usually at this time he went back to the hen house where, if Henrietta was out getting breakfast, he could sometimes find an empty perch on which he could snooze for another hour or two undisturbed. But this morning he had a scheme.

I guess nobody will be surprised to learn that it was a scheme by which he hoped to get together an audience to listen to one of his speeches.

He rapped on the door with his beak—tap, tap, tap.

He heard the bed creak, and a sleepy voice said, "Go away; I'm busy."

"Oh, get up! Get up!" said Charles impatiently. "You ought to be ashamed to lie there in bed when everybody else has been up for hours."

There was a sound of movement inside, then the door opened and Freddy stood there rubbing his eyes. "If you've been up for hours, I'll eat my Webster's Dictionary," he said. "Leaf by leaf." Then he yawned. "Eeeeee-*yaw*! Might not be bad, at that," he said, "if you put on plenty of sugar and cream. Well, come in. What's poisoning your mind so early in the morning?"

"I've got an idea, Freddy—a great idea," said Charles. "After you went to bed early last night Jinx was telling us all about those Winches and Mr. Camphor and—well, this is what I thought. Why don't you invite all the animals to a lecture tonight? You tell 'em what happened—it's as exciting as anything! You can type out a notice and post it up—something like this: 'Free Lecture

Tonight in the Barn. The Inside Story of the Great Camphor Case.' No, that isn't good. 'Among the Savage Winches of Our Northern Frontier.' That'll get 'em out. 'By Freddy, the Intrepid Explorer.' Eh? How's that? Maybe you could even charge admission."

Freddy had sat down in his big chair, and he continued to yawn without paying a great deal of attention. "Yeah?" he said indifferently. "And what's the rest of it?"

"The rest of it?" Charles repeated.

"Yes. Where do you come in?"

"Oh—me!" Charles waved a deprecatory claw. "I'd just—well, I'd just introduce you. Give you a good send-off, you know."

"Doesn't seem to me I need much of an introduction to most of the animals on this farm," said Freddy. "Having lived here all my life. And then, I know your introductions, rooster. Meeting begins at eight. Singing the national anthem: eight to eight-ten. Introduction of principal speaker by Charles: eight-ten to ten-twenty-nine. Lecture: ten-twenty-nine to ten-thirty. Lights out: ten-thirty. No, no, my boy. You call your meeting and make your own speech and lecture and all of it. I've got too much to do today to bother, anyway."

"But nobody will come if I'm the only one that's going to talk," Charles protested.

"That's why I won't go and give a lecture," said Freddy. And as Charles only looked puzzled, he said, "Oh, figure that out for yourself."

Charles looked rather unhappy. "What's the matter with my speeches anyway, Freddy?" he asked. "They're good—I *know* they're good. People cheer and clap when I make 'em. And yet, they never want to come hear 'em."

"Well," said Freddy, "I guess the trouble is that it's so easy for you to make a speech that you never bother to try to have something to say. You use fine big words and beautiful figures of speech. But you've heard the saying, 'Fine words butter no parsnips,' haven't you?"

"Pooh!" said Charles. "Who likes parsnips?"

"But the trouble is," said Freddy, "that all your fine words are just decorations around big pieces of nothing. One of your speeches is like a beautiful frame without any picture in it. It's like a beautiful gold dish without any ice cream in it. It's like—"

"I guess you're making a speech yourself, aren't you?" said Charles sourly.

"Yeah, I am at that," the pig replied. "It kind

of creeps up on you, doesn't it? And I've got to go, too. Got to get up to Camphor's this morning." Then he looked at his crestfallen friend. "Cheer up, Charles. I'd give my bottom dollar to be able to speak as well as you do. That's the trouble. You're *too* good. So good you can even talk about nothing and make it sound all right. The thing for you to do is, be sure you're going to talk about *something*. Then they'll come from miles around to hear you."

As he saw Charles walk away across the barnyard with his tailfeathers drooping disconsolately, Freddy felt a little sorry that he had been so frank. But there was no time to do anything about it now. He had a plan to carry out, and he must get going.

He picked up a big beef bone that he had begged from Mrs. Bean, but just as he was going out of the door he felt a tickle in his right ear, and Mr. Webb's voice said, "Got a minute. Freddy? I want your advice. I started down from the cow barn at two this morning, to catch you before you left, but I got held up. Deputation of squash bugs came over to pledge allegiance. Of course I had to give 'em the oath. So I'm a little late."

"I've got to take this bone up to Johnny," said Freddy. "Why don't you come along? We can talk on the way."

"Fine," said the spider. "Splendid. Just so I can get word to mother—so she won't worry. She's kind of a worrier, Mrs. Webb is."

On the way up to the woods Freddy hailed a rabbit and sent him off with a message to Mrs. Webb. Then as he trotted along he listened to the spider's story.

The Webbs had really done a splendid, patriotic job. Using moths and dragonflies, and occasionally a bird, they had flown over most of the township, organizing and delivering speeches. "You'd be amazed, Freddy, to know how much you can do when you get started. We've trained fifty organizers who go out and speak at different farms, and with their help two hundred and eighteen farms have been canvassed, and between eighty-nine and ninety million bugs have pledged themselves not to eat vegetables for the duration."

"Ninety million!" said Freddy admiringly. "That's an awful lot of bugs."

"Well, they're pretty patriotic, bugs are," said the spider. "And they don't often get a chance to do anything for their country. Of course there's a lot of 'em—perhaps thirty per cent—that don't eat vegetables anyway—us spiders, and dragonflies and such. But they help too—going around and telling others."

"But if some of them can't eat vegetables what are they going to eat?" Freddy asked.

"That's something we're working out now. I want to appoint a committee to scout for other sources of food. Find out where different weeds grow wild—weeds they can eat. I'm going to call it the War Food Production Board, the WFPB. That will have bees on it, and dragonflies—folks that fly long distances all the time. And then there'll be the BTA, the Bug Transportation Administration, which will arrange to carry bugs from where they live near gardens, to places where they will find other food. Oh, it's a complicated business, Freddy. But there's one big headache in it—that Zero."

"What's he up to now?" Freddy asked.

"I guess you didn't see his sign," said the spider. "He wove one yesterday up by the garden, challenging me to a public debate tomorrow night. And to tell you the truth, I don't know what to do about it. I'm not a very good speaker, you know. And he's clever—you've got to admit that. He can talk rings around me. I wondered if you didn't want to come and answer him. It would be a big help."

"I'm not a very good speaker myself," said Freddy. "I'd be glad to, of course, but—" He remembered suddenly the talk he had just had with Charles. "I've got it!" he said. "Charles is your speaker. He's the one you want."

"Oh, Charles!" said Mr. Webb disgustedly. "Lot of high-flown balderdash! You see, Freddy, this won't be a regular debate on the merits of patriotism. This Zero will get personal. He'll attack my character. He'll say that I'm a crook. And you can't meet that kind of thing with big words."

"No," said Freddy, "I agree. But the trouble is, you've heard Charles too often. The first time you heard him you thought he was wonderful. So did all of us. And these bugs will be hearing him for the first time. And there's another thing. I had a talk with him this morning." And he told Mr. Webb what he had said. "Now, you leave it to me," he concluded. "I'll give Charles another going over, and then we'll stuff him full of facts. Not about patriotism—he's got that down pretty well—but about Zero himself. I'll bet he'll make the speech of his life."

"I don't like the idea very well, Freddy," Mr.

Webb said. "But if you say so, we'll try it. After all, there's nobody else."

By this time they had come down into the valley beyond the Big Woods and were approaching the Schemerhorn farm. Beside the gate they saw the black dog, Johnny, and Freddy went up to him.

"Ah, Freddy," said the dog. He sniffed the air eagerly. "That a bone you've got there?"

"Yes. I want to make a deal with you, Johnny. I want to borrow those trained fleas for a couple of days, and in exchange I'll give you this bone. How about it?"

"Well, I don't know," said Johnny slowly. "I ain't ever lent my fleas before. You sure you'd take good care of 'em?"

"Sure," said the pig. "I've got a little job for them. I'll bring them back safe and sound."

"We-ell," said the dog slowly, "I guess maybe . . . Could you make it *two* bones, Freddy? he asked, sniffing greedily. "I ain't had a bone like that in I can't remember when. Never, I guess. Honest, I ain't."

"I'll make it three," said Freddy. "I've only got this one now, but I'll bring you the others later, if you'll trust me."

"It's a deal," said Johnny. "Atten-*tion!*" he

said. "Go over to Freddy, boys. Do as he tells you."

Freddy saw the little black specks hop through the air, and then he felt a sharp tickle in his ear as Mr. Webb moved uneasily about. "Hey," said the spider, "what is this? I'm not particular, but I'm not going to pal around with a gang of fleas. A joke's a joke, but—"

"This isn't a joke," said Freddy. "They won't bother you, Webb. Only stand still, will you? You tickle."

"You'll get tickled, all right," Mr. Webb grumbled, "before you get very far."

But after the dog had instructed Freddy in the proper way to handle the fleas, they behaved pretty well. One or two of the younger and more spirited ones took a nip at the pig, but that was only to be expected. Fleas are so nearly invisible that they find it easy to get away with things that wouldn't be tolerated for a moment in larger creatures. It is pretty hard to catch and punish a flea for bad manners. And so they do about as they please.

When they got to the Camphor estate, Freddy went in the gates and straight down to the entrance to the secret passage. The two toads were sitting by the door of their new home, and Elmo nodded to him, but Waldo turned his back.

Freddy spoke to them pleasantly. "I hope to have some good news for you a little later," he said.

"Oh, I hope so," said Elmo. "We don't like this new place at *all*. Terribly dry, and hardly a bug.—There, Waldo," he said sharply. "There's one!"

"Oh, shut up; I see him!" said Waldo crossly, as a small fly with gauzy wings came fluttering past them. Waldo didn't move, even his eyes didn't move, but as the fly came closer, suddenly, the toad's tongue shot out and in again, so quickly that Freddy could hardly see it. And the fly was gone.

"Golly," said Freddy. "Pretty neat, eh, Webb?"

"I'll say," replied the spider. "Wish mother could have seen that. Make her pretty sick, though—thinking of all the time she has to spend spinning fly nets, when these boys can catch 'em as easy as that."

"Well, I must get along," said Freddy. "Maybe you two can move back to your old home tonight."

"Where have I heard that before?" said Waldo sarcastically.

Freddy went through the passage and up into the attic. He stuck his head inside the door and called several times for Simon, but nobody answered. "I wonder if they've gone?" he thought; but no, some more chewing had been done on Mr. Camphor's ancestors. "Well, I guess we can get them out," he said. "Atten-*tion!*"

The fleas lined up in front of him on the attic floor. Then when he had given them their instructions, he said: "All right, fleas. Go in and take 'em."

The fleas vanished. For perhaps five minutes there wasn't a sound. Then from dark corners and from under the floor came a rustling and a scampering and a squeaking that grew louder and louder until at last one, and then another, and then half a dozen rats came dashing out, jumping and squealing and turning somersaults in the effort to get away from the fleas who were biting them unmercifully.

Freddy watched them for a minute, then he said: "Atten-*tion!*" again as Johnny had taught him, and in five seconds the fleas were all lined up in front of him again, and the rats, looking rather dazed, ran back out of sight.

Freddy stepped out into the middle of the attic. "Well, Simon," he called, "do you want to

Freddy watched them for a minute . . .

come out and talk business, or shall I send my little friends in after you again?"

Simon came slowly out and faced the pig. "What do you think you're trying to do?" he snarled angrily. "Try that again and I'll set the boys on you! You're surrounded right now, pig, and if I give the word they'll tear you to pieces."

"Oh, shut up, Simon," said Freddy. "If I was alone they could make it pretty hot for me, all right. But I'm not alone. Still, if you want to try it," he said, "go ahead. But I ought to warn you that these fleas have only been playing with you so far. They're a picked outfit, and if they really go to work on you, I don't think you and your boys will have much time over to fight me."

Simon knew perfectly well that this was true and he changed his tune. "What do you want to get so tough for, Freddy?" he whined. "We haven't done you any harm, and we don't want to either. Why can't you let us live here quietly—"

Freddy interrupted him. "I told you last time I was here," he said, "that if you wanted to live here quietly, without destroying property, I wouldn't do anything about it. But you've got this attic in a worse mess than it was before. You've chewed up some more of the pictures, and look at these clothes—and the holes in those boxes. No, Simon, you've had your chance. Now listen to me. You're moving out right now, bag and baggage. And you're staying out. I don't care where you go, but if you try to come back again you'll be sorry. Because I'm coming back here every day or so, and if I find you here I'll turn the fleas on you again. And this time I'll tell them to stay with you. And how would you like that?"

Simon didn't say anything, but his quick little eyes darted from side to side of the attic, and then he gave a sharp squeal and jumped at Freddy. And from under furniture, and from the dark corners the rats darted out to the attack.

Chapter 16

But Freddy had been ready for them. "Go for
'em, fleas!" he shouted. "Drive 'em! Drive 'em
down the passage!"

He sidestepped Simon's rush and smacked
him with the swing of a fore trotter that made
the old rat's head swim. Zeke, the largest of the
rats, had jumped for Freddy's back, and his
brother, Ezra, had attacked from the rear. But
Freddy whirled, knocking Ezra over with his
snout, then rolled, pinning Zeke under him.

And by that time the fleas had gone into action. Not another rat paid the slightest attention to Freddy. They whirled and jumped and squealed in the wildest confusion, but gradually, one after another, fled out the door into the passage. Even Zeke, who had had the wind knocked out of him, got up and staggered whimpering after them.

"Nice going," remarked Mr. Webb. He had prudently woven a few strands with which he had lashed himself securely to Freddy's ear, and so had managed not to get shaken off when the pig rolled over. "I didn't know you were such a fighter, Freddy."

The fleas were herding the rats down the passage as dogs drive a flock of sheep. "It's all over now, I guess," said Freddy, following along.

When they came out on the bank of the creek, some of the rats started upstream and others down, but Freddy shouted his orders, and the fleas headed them back and right down into the water. Then they lined up in front of Freddy again.

Freddy thanked them warmly; then, when the last rat had disappeared, wet and shivering, in the underbrush across the creek, he took them aboard again. They were starting homeward when the two toads hopped up.

"My, Freddy, that was wonderful," said Elmo. "I guess we owe you an apology."

"That's all right," said Freddy. "I guess they won't give us any more trouble."

"Well, if there's ever anything we can do for you," said Elmo, "we'd be only too glad."

"Why, thanks," said Freddy. He looked at them thoughtfully. "Now I come to think of it," he said, "there is something."

"I knew it!" said Waldo.

"How would you like to come down to the farm for a few days as my guest?" Freddy asked. "Then we can talk it over and see if it will work out. Anyway, you'll get some fun out of it, and I'll bring you back whenever you want to come."

Elmo thought this was a fine idea, but of course Waldo didn't, and they argued about it until finally Freddy said: "Well, I can't stay here all day. And as I'd only need one of you, you come along, Elmo, and Waldo can stay here."

"That's right," said Waldo bitterly. "Go off and leave me here all alone!"

Mr. Webb had heard the conversation of course, and now he said in Freddy's ear: "Agree with him, pig. You can make him do anything by always taking his side of the argument away from him."

Freddy hadn't thought of this before, but he thought he'd try it, and he said: "I don't suppose Waldo would have much fun there anyway."

"How do you know I wouldn't?" demanded the toad.

"No," continued Freddy, "you'd have a lot better time here. It's no fun traveling around a lot of strange places. Of *course* you don't want to go."

"I do too want to go!" said Waldo.

"Then hop on my back," said Freddy, bending down quickly, and presently Waldo, much to his surprise, found himself riding beside his brother up the drive towards the gates.

"That was wonderful, Webb," said Freddy. "How'd you ever think of it?"

"I've had a lot of experience lately with contradictors," said the spider. "At these meetings. Whole audiences sometimes go contrary on you. And I've found this usually works. When they start going in the wrong direction, you kind of lead 'em in a circle, and pretty soon they're going along your way without realizing it."

"Who are you talking to?" asked Elmo, who had heard Freddy speak, and of course couldn't see the spider.

So Freddy explained about Mr. Webb.

"Spiders are no good," said Waldo.

"How right you are," said Freddy, who thought he would like to try out these new tactics and see how they worked. "Mean, cranky creatures, they are," he continued. "I've half a mind to pitch this one off and leave him up here, so I won't ever have to see him again."

"Why don't you pick on somebody your own size?" said Waldo. "According to your story, this spider is a friend of yours. That's a fine way to treat a friend."

"No friend of mine," said Freddy. "Pitch him out of my ear, will you?"

"I will not!" Waldo retorted. "And you leave him alone. I won't have him picked on."

Freddy could hear Mr. Webb giggling. Then the spider said: "This looks like the beginning of a beautiful friendship, Freddy. But keep it up. You've got the trick of handling him now."

They went on down, and Freddy turned the fleas over to Johnny again, and then they continued over the hill and through the Big Woods. When they got home, Freddy found a nice damp hole for the toads to stay in. It was near the brook, and Mr. Webb recommended it highly as one of the coziest and buggiest places on the farm. Waldo objected to it, of course; but when

Freddy agreed that it was entirely unsuitable, the toad insisted that it was probably the best place they were likely to find, and refused to look further.

Freddy got down to the barnyard to find the sheriff sitting on the back porch talking to Mr. Bean. When he saw the pig, the sheriff waved and walked over to him.

"Came up to talk to you a minute," he said. "The Winch case is all settled, and Mr. Camphor wants you to come back and take your job again."

"Well, I don't know that I want to do that," said Freddy. "It's a nice place all right, but Mr. Camphor was pretty quick to believe that I was a thief. I wouldn't want to work for anybody that was so suspicious."

"You can't hardly blame him for suspectin' you," said the sheriff. "Things looked pretty black. And he's an awful nice man. He's figured out something I think you'll like."

Freddy asked if the Winches had been put in jail.

"No, Mr. Camphor didn't want to send 'em to jail, so he didn't make any charge against them. He said he'd got back most of the stuff that was stolen, and that was enough. But he's put the

Winches sort of on probation. They're going to stay there for a while and work around the place, and he wants you to come take charge of things. Mrs. Winch, she keeps her cookin' job same as before, and she'll cook your meals. And it'll be up to you to see that Mr. Winch and Horace behave themselves. I guess he sort of figures that Horace ought to have a chance to be with somebody besides his father. He thinks the boy might be all right if anybody showed him—well, how to act, and how to have some real fun that wasn't stealin' and destroyin' things. He thought maybe you could do it."

"Me?" said Freddy. "I wouldn't be a very good example. I'm kind of greedy, I guess, and I know I'm lazy, and—and—oh, my goodness, I wouldn't want to feel that I had to go around acting just the way I *ought* to act all the time. It would be a terrible strain."

"Well, of course that isn't the idea, and you know it," said the sheriff. "You're just making up excuses. But think it over. I must be getting on. Drop down to the jail some day. Joe, the Gimp, has invented a new kind of ice cream, and the prisoners are all crazy about it. I'd like you to try it. Well, so long."

Freddy went over to the pigpen and spent the

rest of the afternoon typing out a lot of notices for Mr. Webb. Then he and the spider went over and had a long talk with Charles.

The meeting that evening was probably the largest ever held by bugs in the United States. The debate between Zero and Mr. Webb had been well advertised, and had aroused much interest; and every bug who could get there was present. Many of them of course could not fly, and had to walk or crawl, but fleets of dragonflies belonging to the BTA had been making trips all afternoon to the more remote parts of the farm, and even to neighboring farms, to bring in those for whom the distance was too great. Freddy had made a new and larger megaphone for the occasion, and several crews of ants had been working all day leveling and smoothing a space in front of it as big as your living-room floor. And when Mr. Webb climbed up that evening to the speaker's stand—which was just the little space inside the paper cone at the small end —he faced an audience which was estimated later at something over fifteen thousand.

With so large a crowd, it had been impossible to arrange things so that those in the side seats could see the speaker. Those in the middle, however, could see him plainly, for a large number of fireflies had been stationed on top of the mega-phone, and the light came right through the paper and made a soft and pleasant glow of in-direct lighting. And of course as the megaphone was so large, everyone could hear perfectly.

Mr. Webb spoke first. The agreement was, he said, that he would first speak for five minutes, and then Zero would speak for five minutes. After that, each would have another five min-utes to answer the other's arguments. "But as you know," he said, "I am no silver-tongued orator. I believe in the work which I have been doing, I believe that with your cooperation we can make a great contribution to the war effort. But there are others who can explain my reasons for believing that better than I can. And I have asked one such person to speak here in my place tonight. I think he needs no introduction to most of you. And in order not to waste what re-mains of my first five minutes, I will now turn the meeting over to him."

A row of fireflies ranged along the branch of the tree which overhung the audience turned on their lights at this and revealed Charles perched there.

"My friends," said the rooster, "the question before us tonight seems to be whether, as my friend Webb claims, it is your patriotic duty to give up eating vegetables for the duration, or whether, as that rabble-rousing nuisance, Zero, asserts, it is all silly nonsense."

At this point he was interrupted. Zero, buzzing angrily, flew into the megaphone, knocking Mr. Webb off his feet, and shouted: "Who says I'm a nuisance? What kind of a debate is that? What right has this long-legged feather duster to stick his beak into this meeting anyway?" And he went on like this for a minute or two.

But the audience didn't like it. "Shut up!" they shouted. "Throw him out!" And those that could hiss, hissed. And Zero, who was no fool, saw that he was just making himself unpopular, so he stopped talking. But he stayed inside the megaphone.

"My hysterical opponent," Charles resumed, "has now used up one minute of the five allotted to him. I should like to point out to him that in a political debate of this nature, calling names is entirely permissible. He will have four minutes at the end of my speech in which to call me all the names he can think of, and if he can't think of enough, I will be glad to lend him some of those I have thought up for him; for I assure you, my friends, that I could call him unpleasant names from now to midnight—and all of them would be true."

The audience laughed at this, and Zero buzzed angrily, but Charles went on.

"However, my friends, this fly, this sour-faced, buzzing nitwit, is of no importance. What is important tonight is the facts. And let me give you a few." Whereupon, for the first time in his career as a speaker, Charles attempted to back up his oratory with facts and figures. He gave the number of tons of vegetables which the Victory Gardens of New York State were expected to produce. Then he gave, in ounces, the amount which the average bug would eat during the summer, and multiplying that by seventy trillion, the estimated number of vegetable eating bugs in the state, arrived at the amount of destruction which bugs would do to the crop. Of course it is doubtful if any of his audience understood his figures, for bugs are not much good at arithmetic; nevertheless his show of knowledge made a great impression. He stopped speaking amid universal applause.

Then Zero took the platform. All these figures, he said, didn't mean a thing. "How does this smart-aleck rooster know that there are seventy trillion bugs in New York State?" he demanded. "Has he counted them? Has anybody counted them? Ridiculous! Do you know, my friends, how long it would take merely to count up to seventy trillion? Hundreds and hundreds of years! No, no, my friends, you are not as gullible as that!

"And let me ask you this: why, if these figures are any good, doesn't old Webb give them to you himself? Why does he get this loud-mouthed bunch of feathers, this bird who can't even fly, to speak for him? I will tell you. It is because he is ashamed to come before you with such a lot of idiotic statements. For even a spider, we must suppose, has some small measure of self-respect. Again I say to you: no! There is no sense to be found in any of this stuff."

And then he went on to attack Charles's character. Some of the things he said, Freddy thought, were rather good. Charles, he said, was nothing but a feathered alarm clock, and not even a good one—a false alarm, rather. He had a fine loud voice, but so had a drum, so had an empty barrel. The emptier a thing was, the louder the sound it made. And so on.

Freddy was pleased, and somewhat surprised, to see how well Charles kept his temper. He clucked indignantly a few times at some of the meaner digs, but until Zero's five minutes were up he didn't say a word.

But when his turn came, he tore into the fly with all the eloquence at his command. His audience would know, he said, how much weight to give to the words of a multiple-eyed loafer who had never done an honest day's work in his life. "He talks of emptiness," said Charles. "He compares me to barrels and drums. But I ask you, my friends, to consider his name. Zero! Nothing, surrounded by a small black line! How well it fits him! How perfectly it describes him! And yet it is he—this flying cipher, this bumbling incompetent who will one day meet a deserved fate at the business end of a fly swatter— it is he who dares to tell you that your patriotism is ridiculous and useless." He lowered his voice dramatically. "But, my friends, you are too clever to be taken in by such empty tirades. Whatever my seditious and deluded opponent may say to the contrary, we are still all good Americans.

"Are we not?" he shouted suddenly, and in his claw appeared a small American flag, which he had borrowed from Mrs. Bean, and which he now waved above his head.

The audience broke into wild cheering. It was plain to everybody that Zero had lost the debate; it was plain even to Zero, for instead of coming forward for the five minutes of speech now allotted to him, he buzzed down among the audience, knocking the smaller bugs right and left.

"I'll show you who's boss around here!" he cried shrilly. "No spider is going to run this show, and no silly rooster either!" And he skated around wildly among the terrified audience, who ran and hopped and crawled for cover as fast as they could.

Freddy had rather expected something like this. The trouble with Zero, he realized, wouldn't end with the debate, even if the fly were defeated. After this, Mr. Webb would never be able to hold a peaceful meeting anywhere on the farm. Stern measures were called for if the patriotic program was to be saved. And fortunately Freddy was prepared to take them.

"Hey, Zero," he called. "Why don't you pick on somebody your own size?"

The fly paused and looked up. "Ha, pig!" he exclaimed. "I told you we'd meet again, didn't I? All right, let's see what *you* can do." And he rose and circled above Freddy's head. "I bet I make *you* yell uncle!"

Freddy just laughed. "With that weak little

sting of yours? Pooh, you couldn't even make a mouse jump!"

Now if there is one thing a horsefly prides himself on, it is his ability to bite. And indeed his bite is nothing to laugh at. Even a horse will jump and kick when a horsefly bites him.

"Go on, fly," Freddy said. "Light right on my nose, and then do your worst. I'm going to show you up, you big blowhard!"

Freddy was lying down with his nose along the ground, but close to his nose, one on each side, were Elmo and Waldo. "Oho!" said Zero. "Well, you asked for it, pig." And he laughed his unpleasant laugh and settled right on the end of Freddy's nose. And the toads, who were squatting down under the tangle of grass stems, he never saw at all.

Freddy clenched his teeth. "Do your stuff," he said, and Zero laughed again.

"Don't you worry," he said menacingly.

But of course Freddy's remark had been addressed to the toads, who he hoped would surely do their stuff before Zero got to work. And they did. Flick—flick! their two tongues shot out like two electric sparks . . . and the fly vanished.

Even though Freddy was so close to them he didn't know which one had caught Zero. The fly

. . . and settled right on the end of Freddy's nose.

had been there—and then he had vanished.

The audience had been craning their necks and climbing on top of one another to see what had happened. And when nothing happened, they thought that the fly had given up and flown away, and they began to yell and make fun of him. For none of them had seen the toads.

Freddy didn't want them to see the toads, for the presence of a toad at a bug party can easily start a panic. But Charles almost gave the trick away. For he flapped his wings for attention, and said: "And that, my friends, is the end of Zero. So perish all traitors!"

"Yes," said Freddy quickly, "that is the end of him. And now, Charles, since you have unquestionably won the debate, perhaps you have a few more words to say."

And as all eyes were again turned towards the rooster, he got up, and the toads, without being seen, hopped after him down to the pigpen.

Chapter 17

Freddy had been undecided as to whether he should go back to take his job with Mr. Camphor again or not. But the next morning Mr. Camphor himself drove into the yard. And he apologized so handsomely in the presence of the entire barnyard that Freddy decided to go back with him. So he said goodbye to his friends, and he and Elmo and Waldo got into the back seat of the car, and they drove off.

Elmo was in the best of spirits, but Waldo

wasn't feeling very well. The corners of his wide mouth seemed to turn down more than usual, and he kept swallowing every minute or so, and after a while he got the hiccups.

"Darned fly!" he grumbled. "Don't know why I ever agreed to catch him in the first place!"

"Oh, it was you that got him, was it?" said Freddy. "Well, I'm pretty grateful, Waldo, and so is Webb."

"That don't make my stomach feel any better," said Waldo.

So Freddy didn't say any more.

Freddy had lunch with Mr. Camphor in the big dining room, and during the meal nothing was said about business. Bannister, who waited on them, suggested a number of proverbs which they discussed. They found that it was true that "You can't have your cake and eat it too," for they tried it out several times on a large chocolate cake that Mrs. Winch had baked for dessert. Indeed, they tried it out so thoroughly that there was none left for Bannister, who remarked rather glumly that apparently he couldn't have it or eat it either.

After lunch they went down to where Mr. Winch and Horace had been set to work cleaning up the houseboat. They stood on the bank and watched them for a while. And then Mr. Camphor said:

"I'm putting you in charge of those two, Freddy. They will mow the lawn and rake leaves and do whatever work is necessary to keep the place looking nice. You won't have any trouble with them, for their jail sentence has only been suspended, and they know that if you complain about them, the sheriff will come up and take them away.

"Now there's one other thing I want to speak to you about, and that's that portrait."

"Let me tell you about that, Mr. Camphor," said Freddy. And then he told him the whole story, about finding the secret passage, and the rats, and how later he had gone in the house to try to frame Mr. Winch, and had been caught as a burglar.

Mr. Camphor wasn't as much surprised as Freddy had thought he would be. "I had an idea something like that had happened," he said. "But what I wanted to say was: I've been up and looked at those portraits. I felt pretty bad when I saw what the rats had done. But you did so well with the one you repaired that I wondered if you wouldn't want to tackle the others? Of course I wouldn't want them all painted with their vizors

down, and of course you couldn't anyway, because most of them aren't in armor. What do you
think you could do?"

Freddy said he thought he could fix them.
He'd look them over . . .

They were interrupted by a terrible splash
and, looking around, saw that Horace who had
been scrubbing paint on the railing, had fallen
into the creek. The water wasn't deep, but even
half an inch of water would have terrified
Horace, and Freddy ran down and pulled him
out, while Mr. Winch looked on without much
interest.

Horace was all right, but of course he was wet
all over, which was something that hadn't happened to him in a long long time. And he sat
down on the bank and burst into tears.

"Well," said Mr. Camphor, "I have to get
back to Washington tonight, so I must get along.
I'll be up again in another month. Goodbye, and
if anything goes wrong, just call the sheriff."
And he shook hands with Freddy and left.

Freddy went over to Horace. "Come on," he
said. "Come into the houseboat and we'll dry
you off."

So Freddy took him into the bathroom, and
while he was working over him with a towel,

Horace caught sight of himself in the mirror. "Why!" he exclaimed. "I—why, I look real nice!" For of course he had never really seen himself before; all he had seen was the dirt on his face.

"Of course you look nice," Freddy said. "And you'll look nicer when I've got through with you." And he soaped a washcloth, without letting Horace see what he was doing, and washed the boy's face.

Well, Horace was delighted. He couldn't stop admiring himself in the mirror, but finally he went outdoors again. And Mr. Winch saw him.

"Who—who's this?" he demanded. He peered sharply at the boy. "It's not—it can't be—Horace?"

"Sure, it's me, pa," said Horace. "Don't I look nice?"

"Nice!" exclaimed Mr. Winch in horror. "You look—you look terrible!" And he put his hands over his face and sank down in a chair. "All my teaching!" he moaned. "All the trouble I've had in bringing you up to be a true son of your father! And what have you done? You've thrown it away for a cake of soap! You've sold your birthright for a lot of cold water!"

Nobody said anything, and pretty soon Freddy

remarked that Mr. Winch was peeking through his fingers. And after a little longer he took his hands down entirely and stared at his son. And as he stared, he seemed to be getting angry, and at last he burst out.

"So!" he said. "Trying to shame your pore old dad, are you? His ways aren't good enough for you, eh? Want to have a clean shirt every Sunday, I expect!"

"I'm not trying to shame you, pa," said Horace. "It's just—just—I didn't know that being clean was so comfortable."

"Why don't you try it, Mr. Winch?" said Freddy. "Of course it takes a lot of nerve. Soap, now. That's something that's pretty hard to face. Horace is a pretty brave boy."

"He ain't any braver'n his pa, I should hope," said Mr. Winch aggressively.

"Well, I don't know. I didn't use to think so, but—"

"Oh," said Mr. Winch, "you think I can't take it, hey? Well, we'll see about that." And he rushed into the bathroom.

"My goodness," Freddy thought, "that's the same trick I worked with Waldo. Maybe Mr. Winch will be just as easy as that."

And oddly enough, that was about the way it

worked out. In a week Horace and Mr. Winch had been cleaned up so that they were quite presentable. Even Mrs. Winch was impressed.

"I don't know how you did it," she said to Freddy. "I guess I got to change my mind about pigs. Not that you'll ever get Zebedee Winch really clean. He's what I might call just naturally sort of dingy anyway. But I'm certainly grateful about Horace. Maybe we can make something of him after all."

After this it wasn't so hard to get Horace interested in painting. Freddy had Mr. Winch bring all the pictures down from the attic, and when the holes had been patched he set to work on them. He let Horace help him, a little at first, but as the boy showed an unexpected talent for painting, Freddy eventually turned some of the work entirely over to him. Mr. Winch objected a good deal in the beginning, but Freddy had found out how to manage him now, and soon he began to be proud of the boy's ability. A chip of the old block, he said; and Freddy agreed.

When Mr. Camphor returned at the end of the month there were six finished portraits to show him. Mr. Camphor and Bannister examined them together.

"What do you think, Bannister?" Mr. Camphor asked at length.

"Well, sir," said Bannister, "anybody would know whose ancestors they are, all right. Quite a remarkable resemblance to you in all of them, if I may say so, sir."

"If you may say so! If you may say so! Ha, you'd better not say anything else!" Mr. Camphor exclaimed. "Why, confound it, Bannister, they're the *image* of me! They don't merely look like my ancestors; they *are* my ancestors! They must be." He stared at them with a sort of delighted amazement. "Seems impossible. But it's true." He turned to Freddy. "You know, they're just a lot of old portraits I bought because I thought it would be fun to name them and hang them up as my ancestors. I didn't want to fool anybody with them. But now—well, I'd be fooling people if I said they weren't my ancestors now. Why, look at the Reverend Wilberforce. Ha! Isn't that me to the life?" He was quite pink with pleasure.

Freddy didn't quite know what to say. Since most of the faces had been gnawed away, he hadn't had any idea what they had looked like, and so when he had put the new faces in he had

"Why, look at the Reverend Wilberforce."

242]   *Freddy and Mr. Camphor*

just copied the big crayon portrait of Mr.
Camphor which stood on the easel in the houseboat. With the result that they were rather like
the row of photographs that he had noticed
when he first took the houseboat over. They
were just portraits of Mr. Camphor in different
fancy costumes.

But it didn't seem quite fair not to tell Mr.
Camphor the truth, so Freddy told him.

And Mr. Camphor was delighted. He thought
it was a wonderful joke, and insisted on hanging
them at once in the dining room. And then he
went from one to another, standing in front of
them with a small mirror in which he com-
pared his own features with those painted on
the canvas, and laughing delightedly. He could
hardly be coaxed away from them to eat his
dinner.

Later he said to Freddy: "I can't tell you how
happy I am that I got you as my caretaker here.
And I don't regret any of the trouble we had,
either—and I hope you don't. For you've worked
wonders with Horace, and even Mr. Winch
seems to be much less objectionable. I'm sure I
don't know how you do it."

"I suppose you'd laugh, Mr. Cam—I mean,
Jimson," said Freddy, "if I told you that it was a

hoptoad who taught me how to get along with difficult people. But it's so." And he told him about Elmo and Waldo.

"You ought to write a book about it," said Mr. Camphor enthusiastically. "Ha—certainly you should write a book. Eh, Bannister?"

"There is no friend like a good book," said Bannister.

"Very true," said Mr. Camphor. "But I didn't ask you for a proverb, I asked you for an opinion."

"But it's the same thing, sir. This book would be a friend because it would tell you how to make friends."

"I think that is a little farfetched," said Mr. Camphor. "But anyway, Freddy, you write your book. And if you—if you—" He stopped and blushed, which was so unusual that Bannister entirely forgot to provide even a very slight amount of dignity and stared with his mouth open.

"If you wish to," went on Mr. Camphor, "you might—ha, you might dedicate it to me. It would please me very much."

So Freddy said he would be glad to. And that very evening he started the book. This was the title:

THE CARE AND MANAGEMENT
OF FRIENDS

A PRACTICAL GUIDE *to the Selection and Training of Likely Prospects, with* SUPPLEMENTARY NOTES *on How to Influence Unpleasant People, and a* BRIEF ACCOUNT *of Some Illuminating Personal Experiences.*

I'm afraid it sounds rather dull, and indeed if Freddy had written it according to the title, I am sure it would have been. But although he started with that idea, pretty soon he did what a good many authors do—he began putting in more and more about himself, until when he had finished it was really not a guide to making friends at all, but a complete autobiography. So that when Mr. Dimsey printed it for him, at the printing office in Centerboro where he printed the *Bean Home News*, he had to change the title. So it came out as

THE LIFE AND TIMES OF FREDDY

by HIMSELF

which was much more interesting all around. For after all, what a person did is usually a lot more interesting than what he thought about it.

And if you would like to read the book you might try your public library.